PIRATES & SCALLYWAGS

A Tale of Adventure, Plunder & Debauchery

SAM STOUTMAN

All rights reserved. No part of this document may be reproduced or transmitted in any form or by any means, electronic, mechanical, photocopying, recording or otherwise, without prior written permission of the publisher, except for the use of brief quotations in a book review or in cases of certain non-commercial uses permitted by copyright law.

Printed in the United States of America.

First Printing, 2018.

ISBN: 978-1-7329131-0-3

Any references to historical events, real people, or real places are used fictitiously. Names, characters, and places are projects of the author's imagination. Any similarity to real persons is coincidental and not intended by the author.

www.piratesandscallywags.com

Copyright © 2018 Sam Stoutman

All rights reserved.

CONTENTS

Part 1: Umberland

CHAPTER ONE 1
CHAPTER TWO 13
CHAPTER THREE 33
CHAPTER FOUR 37

Part 2: Estevez

CHAPTER FIVE 47
CHAPTER SIX 51
CHAPTER SEVEN 55

Part 3: Montpellier

CHAPTER EIGHT 71
CHAPTER NINE 81
CHAPTER TEN 87
CHAPTER ELEVEN 97

Part 4: Borracho

CHAPTER TWELVE 109
CHAPTER THIRTEEN 119
CHAPTER FOURTEEN 135

Part 5: Nature's Fury

CHAPTER FIFTEEN 149

CHAPTER SIXTEEN 159

CHAPTER SEVENTEEN 165

CHAPTER EIGHTEEN 171

CHAPTER NINETEEN 181

Part 6: Paying For Past Sins

CHAPTER TWENTY 187

CHAPTER TWENTY-ONE 193

CHAPTER TWENTY-TWO 199

Part 7: Pirate's Life

CHAPTER TWENTY-THREE 211

CHAPTER TWENTY-FOUR 225

CHAPTER TWENTY-FIVE 233

CHAPTER TWENTY-SIX 241

CHAPTER TWENTY-SEVEN 249

Part 1:
Umberland

PAGE INTENTIONALLY LEFT BLANK

CHAPTER ONE

"Run 'em down Jenkins!" Captain Umberland said to the man at the helm, the sails of their prey visible ahead. "Ready the cannons and muskets lads; we're going hunting!"

The pirate ship *Grog Hog* surged forward, her sails out full. The ship was stripped of anything unnecessary and modified for both speed and resiliency, making her a formidable vessel.

Umberland gripped the rail and leaned in, practically pushing the ship on. This was the part he loved most—the adrenaline kicking in as the chase commenced, the ship rushing forward, the gap between the two vessels narrowing, the wind blasting over the deck, the seawater crashing over the sides; this was what he lived for!

"Hoist the colors high!" he yelled to First Mate Wilcox, thrilled every time he said it.

The cry was repeated by Wilcox to the man responsible, who pulled the rope vigorously. The flag rose to the top, the wind expanding it to full prominence.

Breaking his steely gaze on the ship they were stalking, Captain Umberland cast his eyes up the main mast. Flying above the ship was the flag that he and the crew had designed.

It was black with a red diamond in the middle. Inside the diamond was a skeleton holding a skull in his left hand and a sword in his right. Above his head to the left was an hourglass, while above it to the right was a tankard of beer. The sword represented the crew's willingness to fight. The skull illuminated that those facing them would be shown no mercy. The hourglass signified the unstoppable march of time and was a reminder of mortality. The tankard stood for the importance of celebrating life with friends. Finally, the red diamond represented the four corners of the compass, stating to all that the crew were masters of the world's oceans.

"Pirates!" the man in the ship's Crow's Nest screamed, pointing to the vessel bearing down on them.

Shouts and curses broke out on the deck of the merchant ship *Pride of London*, as the crew watched the ship flying the black flag rapidly approach. When the two vessels were almost level, four of the *Grog Hog's* 30 cannons blasted a warning shot just behind the fleeing vessel.

"Surrender or die!" came the shout from the pirate vessel.

"No mercy to resisters!" another voice rang out, followed by multiple people screaming in unison, "No mercy!"

To the pirates' surprise, the *Pride of London* veered left and smashed into them. Guns mounted on her deck rained shot onto the deck of the *Grog Hog*, the multiple little iron balls forming a blanket of death and destruction.

Screaming unmentionable curses, the pirates fired multiple musket rounds at the defenders, while additional members of the crew secured hooks and planks to the vessel. The wounded were hustled below deck as several pirates rushed over the planks and spread out across the deck, swords at the ready.

Before they could shoot the *Pride of London's* helmsman, he forced the wheel to starboard, moving the ship to the right and separating them. The boarding planks fell between the gap, and the pirates who had already crossed found themselves cut off from reinforcements and outnumbered.

"Death to pirates!" the captain yelled, pulling his sword and leading the armed crew forward to meet the pirates stuck on deck. Sword crashed against sword and knife against knife as the two groups engaged in the ritual dance of death.

Climbing up a pile of crates, Barrel was able to jump from that pile to another, and then down the other side and land right behind Sam. With his back now defended, Barrel aggressively assaulted the two crew members who rounded the pile of crates and quickly defeated them. At the same time, Sam traded blows with two crew members, attempting to maneuver them against the side of the ship.

He let out a scream as one of them pierced his upper arm. Cursing, he leaned against Barrel's back for support and then pushed forward. His momentum enabled him to overpower the man to his left and run him through. He then turned and faced the second man as Barrel moved in to help him. The man fought bravely, but was no match for them.

Up on the Quarterdeck, Franklin, Parrot, Joseph, and three other pirates battled against the ship's captain and most of his officers. Despite being outnumbered, the six of them repeatedly fought off assaults and managed to avoid getting trapped against the railing.

As two of the pirates provided cover on each side, Joseph and Franklin charged three of the men in front of them. Metal crashed against metal as swords flashed in the sunlight. One of the men let out a piercing cry as he fell against Joseph's relentless assault. A deft move by Franklin quickly dispatched another. Rushing to the wheel, he spun it back to port, turning the ship into a slow-moving left turn. Joseph, Parrot, and the three pirates desperately battled against the captain and officers to protect Franklin's control of the wheel.

From the Quarterdeck of the *Grog Hog*, Captain Umberland issued rapid-fire instructions, seeking to capture as much wind as possible and catch up to the *Pride of London*. Witnessing it starting to move left, he hollered at Jenkins to mirror its movement. Struggling on the tossing deck, Jenkins utilized all his strength to steady himself and turn the heavy wooden wheel to port.

Turning in union with it, the *Grog Hog* soon found itself parallel to the ship's deck. Shouting down to the gun deck, Captain Umberland ordered the starboard battery to fire for her mast, rigging and sails.

Onboard the *Pride of London*, Barrel and Sam were fighting their way across the ship towards the Quarterdeck when the roar of cannon fire split the sky and shook the ship. Rigging, bits of cloth, and sections of the mast rained down on the deck as cannonballs and chain-shot smashed through the sails. Combatants on both sides whirled towards the source. The merchant crew's hopes fell while the pirates' hopes rose at the majestic sight of the *Grog Hog* sailing parallel to them, smoke billowing out of her starboard gun ports.

The pirates aboard the *Pride of London* returned their compatriots' shouts and surged forward with renewed vigor. The captain and his officers retreated across the Quarterdeck until they found themselves pressed against the rail, trapped between the advancing pirates in front of them and the cannons of the *Grog Hog* behind them. With the end just seconds away, the captain ordered his men to drop their swords and cease resisting. Franklin yelled out for the remaining crew members to also drop their weapons or be destroyed. Seeing the impossibility of their situation, all complied and the ship was surrendered.

The *Grog Hog* sailed alongside and was secured to it. The pirates boarded and relieved their exhausted companions. Moving across the deck and conducting a quick search of the lower sections, they quickly were in full control.

"Who is in command of this vessel?" Lightning asked while tossing a cannonball from one hand to the other. The crew of the captured ship was assembled in front of him.

"I am," said the 50-year-old captain with a salt-and-pepper beard, stepping forward from the line of people.

A knife flew past his head and slammed into the mast next to him. He and the others stiffened as Barrel walked past them and yanked his knife out of the mast.

"Wrong!" he shouted, gesturing towards the bow. "*That* is who is in command."

A figure in a deep burgundy coat strolled up to the line of captives and said, "Good afternoon, I'm Captain Umberland and these good lads are the pirate crew of the adventure ship *Grog Hog*. Barrel, take a group below and see what goods they have onboard. I want to know what we gained for the trouble we just endured. And to that end, Captain, join me at the bow."

As Barrel and several pirates headed below, Captain Umberland and the ship's captain walked to the bow.

"Tell me Captain, why would you be so stupid as to engage a pirate crew? Do you know what typically happens to those who resist?"

"Indeed I do, more than you'll ever know."

The look in the captain's eyes was something Umberland hadn't been expecting. It was an indescribable mix of pure rage and haunting sorrow.

"Do tell."

The *Pride of London's* captain let out a long, slow sigh. His eyes drifted past Umberland to the water beyond as he said, "My son grew up on the water, just as I did. I used to joke that he was born on it. He had more experience working on a vessel by the time he was 20 than some men twice his age. He became captain of a merchant ship before his 23rd birthday. He was a great captain, a great man. Fair to his crew, loyal to his customers, loving to his family."

The captain's voice drifted off and silence fell between them for a minute.

The sorrow left his voice and anger rose as he continued, "Last year, he was carrying supplies from here in the Caribbean to a customer in London when his ship was attacked by pirates. Despite being brave, he was very smart and knew they were no match. So he ordered the ship to surrender without firing a shot to protect his crew. The scum who boarded tortured every member of the crew and slaughtered them all, my son included. They tied him to the mast and used him for target practice. Just because. Just for some fun. They left one member alive to relay the tale of what had transpired, with the pirate captain declaring, 'I shall never again show quarter to any English dogs.'"

The captain stared straight at Umberland, his last words tragically hanging in the air. Taking a step forward, Umberland patted the man on the shoulder and said, "I'm very sorry for your loss. Most of us pirates are only after plunder and the acquisition of goods. However, there are some who are true devils. Absolute abominations who commit the most heinous deeds for no reason whatsoever. Whether you believe me or not, know that the vast majority of us scallywags truly despise monsters like the one who murdered your son. Do you happen to know his name?"

"Captain l'Olonnais."

"Oh God, worst of the worst. There are many fine French pirates whom I've had the pleasure to either meet or hear about. However l'Olonnais is despised by scallywags the world over due to his complete lack of humanity. He is not a man; he is evil incarnate."

The captain nodded in agreement and said, "To finish answering your question, that is why we resisted instead of surrendering. I vowed I would fight any pirate I ever came across. I should have continued fighting and fell in battle."

Captain Umberland patted him on the shoulder again and assured him that he fought bravely and honored his son properly. There was no need to sacrifice the entire crew to a lost cause. Due to what had transpired with his son, Umberland vowed that no harm would come to him or the crew, so long as they continued to follow instructions. He walked the captain back to where the crew was lined up and ordered medical care be given to those who were wounded. He then proceeded below to join those searching the ship.

In the ship's hold, the pirates discovered a vast array of spices. Parrot opened a bag with "Cinnamon" written on it, stuck his head in, and inhaled deeply. A few of the pirates jumped at the sound of the massive sneeze he let out. A large plume of orange dust rose out of the bag like an angry dragon. Parrot jumped in surprise and reached for his pistol. Sam grabbed his arm and told him to calm down.

"*You* calm down! I *am* calm!" Parrot shouted, pulling away and taking two steps backward. He proceeded to trip over a box and fall backward with a scream, his pistol flying out of his hand.

As the others burst out laughing, Parrot rose cursing. He clenched his fists and took a step forward, but froze when Captain Umberland entered the room and boomed, "What in blazes is going on here!?"

"Captain it was the funniest thing," Sam started to say, before immediately being told to shut up.

For a few seconds nobody spoke. Barrel broke the silence with, "Looks like a haul of spices Cap'n."

"You think so Barrel?"

"No Cap'n. I said it 'looks' like that's all they're carrying. Remember that spice ship we took shortly after we started pirating? We took the cinnamon, vanilla and nutmeg, but left the black pepper bags because it's rather common and wouldn't fetch as much. Then later we were drinking in Barbados... or was it Kingston?"

"What's the point Barrel?" Sam interrupted.

"The *point* is the old sea dog who was at the tavern started laughing when he overheard us talking about the score. Remember what he said? He informed us that spice merchants like to hide gold and silver coins in the bottom of black pepper bags, knowing that pirates often leave those behind because they are less valuable than the other spices."

"And?"

Barrel moved aside and gestured to the bag he had been standing in front of; "Black Pepper" was written down the side.

Barrel looked at Captain Umberland who nodded. Turning to the sack, he pulled out his knife, leaned over and cut a slit in it all the way down. Black pepper spilled onto the floor and spread out like a tattered rug. At the point where the bag ended and the spill began lay three large, brown cloth bags. Picking one up, Barrel shook it vigorously. The sound of coins clinking filled the hold.

The group broke into cheers and took turns patting Barrel on the back.

"Load the coins and the spice bags onto the *Grog Hog*, especially the cinnamon in case Parrot wants to entertain us some more," Captain Umberland said to laughter from all but Parrot. "And give Barrel an extra share of rum!"

Despite objections from some of the pirates, Captain Umberland ordered the crew and captain be left unharmed and allowed to keep the empty vessel. He left them food and water, and instructed the rigging be damaged but not destroyed, to prevent the ship from reaching a port too soon.

With everyone back onboard the *Grog Hog*, Umberland informed Jenkins of their new heading, and the mighty ship turned west, sailing into the setting sun.

Walking onto the Quarterdeck a short while later, Joseph spotted Captain Umberland standing by the railing and delivered to him a cup of the dark, strong tea he preferred.

"Thank you Joseph."

Captain Umberland took a sip and closed his eyes for a half-second, enjoying the delicious combination of the tea's aroma and full-bodied flavor. A small smile appeared on his face as he finished.

"I hope you don't mind me saying, but how come you always smile after taking the first sip Sir?"

"First off, remember what I've told you Joseph; call me 'Captain,' not 'Sir.' 'Sir' makes me feel like one of those horrible people at the counting house I used to work at. As for the tea, well you must do that lad. When you find something you truly enjoy, you must savor it. We never know what tomorrow will bring, so we must enjoy today as much as we can. Do you understand?"

"Savor what we love? Like being in the sack with a harlot?"

Captain Umberland let out a laugh and said, "That's not exactly what I was talking about."

Joseph looked at him a little confused.

"Tell me lad, how did you come to be a sailor?"

"I beg your pardon?"

"When I met you, you were working on the *Bristol*. What made you decide to live a life at sea?"

"I lost a bet."

"You lost a bet?"

"Yeah. I lost a bet and the agreement was that whoever lost had to go to sea."

"And if we hadn't invited you to join us as pirates, you just would have gone on working at sea… forever?"

"I guess so."

"Oh Joseph," Captain Umberland said, patting him on the shoulder.

"What's wrong?"

"Nothing. You did well today during the attack. Go join the others below and get some food and rum."

Captain Umberland watched him walk away and couldn't help but smile. Joseph definitely wasn't the brightest lad, but he was good in a fight and the captain enjoyed having him onboard.

CHAPTER TWO

New Seville was similar to most medium-sized towns in the Caribbean. The mayor, rich merchants, and other well-to-do folk lived "above" the city in the raised section that overlooked the water, while the average folk lived in various sections leading down to the harbor. That section was vigorously attacked by the clergy and pious elite as being a rat's nest of vice and sin. In truth it wasn't all that bad, despite being rough, and was better than other more notorious towns in the Caribbean.

"New Seville ahead!" Sam shouted down from the Crow's Nest, as the lights of the town appeared.

"All right lads just like usual, 10 of you stay on the ship at all times," Captain Umberland said to the assembled crew once they had docked. "Figure out the rotation yourselves. I'm heading to the Crazy Goat with whomever wants to join me."

The crew broke out dice and separated into five groups. In each group, those who threw the lowest scores faced off until only two of them had the absolute lowest score and had to spend the first night guarding the ship.

Lightning, usually a solid thrower, was having a run of bad luck and found himself facing Joseph to determine which of them would have to stay aboard that night. Gathering up the dice, he rubbed them exactly three times between both hands, then spat once over his left forearm. Hurling them onto the deck with a flourish of his right hand, he let out an excited yell as they came to rest showing a higher score. Jumping up, he grabbed his sword and pistols and headed off to join Captain Umberland.

The Crazy Goat was a favorite among pirates. The tavern was originally called Low Tide and served a mix of locals and scallywags. One night the local authorities had shown up to arrest a popular regional pirate named Genarrio. Genarrio was popular because he often shared his spoils with those in need. He was at the tavern drinking when the authorities surprised him and two of his men. They killed one of them and had the upper hand on him when suddenly a goat burst through the door and started destroying everything in its path. Genarrio took advantage of the ruckus, and in between dodging the goat himself, chased off the authorities. The goat broke every bottle in the place, as well as most of the furniture, before bolting out the door as suddenly as it had appeared, never to be seen again. Pirates and locals alike still hike into the hills and make a sport of trying to guess which of the seemingly docile animals is actually the legendary creature.

Afterwards, Genarrio personally paid for the repairs and renamed the place the Crazy Goat in honor of the event. The authorities took the incident as a sign from God and vowed never to return, thus increasing the tavern's appeal to pirates, thieves, adventurers and other interesting characters.

Arriving at the pub, Lightning paused and let out a laugh as he looked up at the famous woodcut sign depicting a kicking goat with two figures fleeing from it. "Ah the old Crazy Goat; it's been too long," he said to himself and entered the premises.

He immediately ducked as a bottle flew over his head, shattering against the partially-opened door behind him. Moving out of the doorway, he watched as the person who threw it got knocked over the head with a chair. "Nice to see nothing's changed!" Lightning said to the person next to him, as two men dragged the dazed man out the door and tossed him into the street.

"Lightning!" a female voice shouted excitedly.

Looking around, he saw the barmaid waving her hand. He made his way over to the bar and flashed her a smile he reserved only for the ladies. "Lupe, beautiful Lupe," he said, softly holding her hand. "It's been far too long since I've seen those gorgeous lips of yours."

Blushing, she pulled her hand away and grabbed him a tankard of beer. Setting it in front of him she said, "Here, put your lips on this."

Grabbing the beer without taking his eyes off her, he replied, "That's not what I want to put my lips on."

Blushing again, she matched him look for look and then headed off to help another customer.

The smile lingered on his face for a second, but immediately disappeared as the dirty, unshaven, overweight man next to him mockingly said, "You can put your lips on me pretty boy."

Lightning jerked his head back and walked quickly away from the bar. The frown on his face eased a bit once he found Captain Umberland, Barrel and Sam sitting at one of the tables in the middle section of the establishment.

"What's wrong?" Barrel asked, seeing the expression on Lightning's face.

"Nothing. There are some strange people here that's all."

All three laughed and agreed.

"Captain, mates, raise 'em up!" Sam said enthusiastically. "Here's to yet another successful haul!"

They clinked tankards, pounded them on the table, and then took long pulls.

Sam, Barrel and Lightning got into an animated conversation about the three years that had passed since they began pirating. After a spell, Captain Umberland downed the rest of his beer in one go, said "*Störtebeker!*", and headed towards the bar.

"You didn't wait for us!" Sam protested.

"You're too slow! Try to keep up whippersnappers!" came the shouted response, half over his shoulder.

Putting his back to the bar, Captain Umberland scanned the room.

The Crazy Goat was a large establishment; upstairs contained eight rooms with plenty of women upon the curved balcony ready to relieve a pirate of his treasure. Stairs ran up either side, with the bar in between. Downstairs was laid out in three levels, each slightly lower than the last. The bar was on the highest section, the door to the establishment and most of the tables were in the middle section, and the dark red booths running along the back wall occupied the lowest section.

"Here you go luv," Lupe said, setting another tankard of beer in front of him.

"Cheers," Captain Umberland replied, laying a few more coins than required on the bar.

"You're a pirate, aren't you?" the man next to him at the bar said.

Umberland gave him a hard look and stayed silent.

"No offense good Sir! I'm quite fond of pirates and always wondered about the chain of events that lead to one turning to it."

"Thinking of becoming a scallywag?"

"No, no, not me. I'm far too mild-mannered for such a life. Just an admirer. You *are* a pirate, right?"

"I am."

"He's a pirate *captain*!" Lupe said from behind them.

The man's eyes opened wide, and he said it was an honor to meet him. "My name is Peter Brickston and I'm from Brighton, England; Brickston from Brighton."

"I'm Captain Umberland from Cumberland, England; Umberland from Cumberland."

The man let out a laugh and they vigorously shook hands.

Umberland invited him back to the table to meet some more pirates. Barrel was quiet and distant, as he often was with new people. Sam and Lightning were more welcoming and engaged him in conversation. He lived an average life as a baker in New Seville. He had been on the island for five years and had a wife and two kids.

After a spell, Sam headed upstairs with one of the wenches, Lightning went to the bar to hang with Lupe, and Barrel was engaged in an animated conversation with a woman at a different table.

"So how did I become a pirate you ask?" Captain Umberland said to Brickston, shifting his head slightly to the right, as was his habit when questioning someone. "Well I didn't choose to live life on the sea; the sea chose me."

Grabbing his tankard, he threw his head back, downing a healthy amount of beer in the process.

Returning the tankard to the table with a thud, he leaned forward and said, "You see, I was once like you, an ordinary man living his life according to the 'rules of society.'"

Here he paused and let out a short laugh, as if spitting an ugly taste out of his mouth.

"One day I returned home from my job at a counting house, worst time of my life. Absolutely horrid place. Miserable people. Soul-sucking work. I tell you, human beings aren't meant to spend their days like that. Sitting in front of a tiny desk all the time, heartless bosses constantly snapping at you, bored out of my mind every day... why did I stay there for two years?!"

Pounding the table, Captain Umberland fired a fierce glare at the memory. Silence engulfed the table; those at the surrounding tables cast short glances in his direction, but said not a word.

"Anyway, one day I returned home after a long day. My wife walked up to me, announced that she was leaving me because I was too nice—too boring—and walked out the door. She had already moved her belongings out while I was at work."

"Wow, that's harsh."

"Yeah, she wasn't a nice person," Captain Umberland said, letting out a humorless laugh. "After she left, I spent all night staring out at the water, just strolling back and forth along the waterfront. I had always dreamt of sea adventures but had never done anything to pursue my dreams. I had just sat in my little house, in my little town, working my little job all my life. Anyway, the night passed, the sun came up, and I headed to work. I was worthless all morning, the boss glaring at me the whole time. Left for lunch at around 11 in the morning. Walked out while he was protesting the time and threatening 'my situation.' Jeeze, what an arse. Anyway, so I'm sitting in a tavern by the water drinking a pint and ignoring my food. I'm staring out the window at the wharf, and that's when it happened. It's like the sea... winked at me."

Looking across the table at Brickston, a smile appeared on Umberland's face.

"I know what you're thinking: *What a load of bunk. What pitiful nonsense.* If I was hearing the story from another, I'd be thinking the same thing. But that's what happened. It's as if the sea called to me; beckoned me. I can't describe it any other way."

Brickston nodded vigorously, not saying a word.

"One minute I was sitting there, not sure what to do next, staring at a completely wrecked life. The next minute I was filled with energy, totally committed to boarding a ship and sailing to parts unknown. Now mind you, I didn't know that the path would lead to piracy; I just knew that I *had* to head off to sea and let the waves carry me where they will. That was three years ago. Ever since that moment, my life's motto has been: *Go where the wind takes me and see what tomorrow brings.*"

Captain Umberland grabbed his tankard and finished it in a mighty pull. Banging it down on the table he shouted, "*Störtebeker!*"

"I like your motto," Brickston said. "Why did you say that word just now?"

"*Störtebeker?* That's a little tradition amongst pirates. We say that name either before or after downing our drinks in one pull. Störtebeker was a famous German pirate who roamed the Baltic Sea between northern Germany and Scandinavia from 1395 to 1400. *Störtebeker* means 'down the mug in one gulp,' and he took that as his pirate name because he was said to be able to down a tankard twice as large as our current ones in one go."

"I like it! Getting back to you, what happened next? How did you go from there to becoming a pirate?"

Wiping the foam off his beard with the back of his arm, Captain Umberland leaned back in his chair and said, "Well first I finished my lunch. Then I headed down to the dock and learned there was a ship sailing to the New World that very afternoon. So I went home, packed a few things, and headed to the counting house. I burst through the door, read my boss the riot act, and stole two bags of coins."

"Really!?"

"Yeah. Screw 'em! Took the smaller bag of coins and gave it to a family of six that were about to lose their home due to a shady loan my boss had made them. First he screwed them over on the terms, then he ordered me to not send the notice of payment due until the day before it was due. Wife had gotten sick, husband was watching the kids, and he wanted to sandbag them so he could get their house after the man was thrown in debtor's prison. This even though my boss was already rich. Absolutely disgusting person."

"That's so vile!"

Umberland nodded and continued, "After dropping the coins off with the family, I went home, grabbed my stuff, headed to the dock and boarded the ship that would carry me to my new life."

"Did you... steal the ship?"

Umberland burst out laughing and said, "God no! I was just sailing on it to the New World. I had absolutely no idea what I would do once I arrived there. However, it was on that ship that I met the lads who became my crew."

"So *how* did you become a pirate?"

"For that story, we'll need more beer. You're behind; drink up lad!"

The man laughed and took a sip from his tankard.

"DRINK!" Umberland roared at him. "If you're going to sit in a scallywag pub with pirates, thieves and whores, you'd better be drinking! Now down it all or be gone!"

The man struggled through laughter and his lack of experience to finish the large tankard, but his will was strong and the beer was emptied.

"Good lad!" Captain Umberland shouted, slapping him heartily on the back. "Hold down the fort while I get more."

Returning with two fresh tankards, Umberland leaned closer and said, "So I'm on the ship carrying me to the New World. The captain is an absolutely ass. Horrifically abuses the crew. Total tyrant. I'm in no mood to talk to the other passengers, so I start hanging around with the crew. I start dining with them and helping out with the chores, mostly just to fuck with the captain."

"He let you do that?"

"Oh he hated it for sure! But I was a passenger so he couldn't force me *not* to do it. He couldn't kick me off the ship, and he couldn't *make* me not do it. He tried, but I just ignored him. After the shit my wife—ex-wife—had just done to me, along with the years of abuse working at the counting house, I simply refused to take his shit. This endeared me to the crew, and some of us became quite close. I told them why I was sailing to the New World and they cracked up at the part where I stole the bags of coins from my old boss. Anyway, late in the trip, we spotted an abandoned ship that pirates had recently attacked and set on fire. The fire wasn't bad enough to sink the ship and there were some items onboard that were valuable, though they didn't appear so. Barrel noticed them and pointed out their value. Our ship's captain came over and threatened to shoot us all. Apparently he wanted the items for himself. When he started to raise his pistol at me, Lightning handed me a knife and I ran him through.

The rest of the lads decided they would rather sail under my command as pirates than spend the rest of their days being worked to death by heartless rich men who didn't give a damn about them. So we took the damaged ship, sailed her to the Caribbean, sold the items, and purchased a new ship that we named the *Grog Hog*. And that Brickston, is the tale of how I turned to piracy," Captain Umberland said, setting down his now-empty tankard.

"Wow! What a story."

"Seems like a lifetime ago. Crazy to think that it's only been three years."

Brickston enjoyed one more tankard with Captain Umberland and then had to call it a night.

As the hour approached two in the morning, Umberland, Sam, Barrel and Lightning found themselves back together at a table in the middle of the pub.

Umberland headed to the bar to get a fresh round of drinks. Walking back to the table, he spotted six men seated at one of the booths in the back. His eyes locked on the man at the center and recognized him instantly—Captain Van Muis of the pirate ship *Devil's Horn*. Umberland and some of the crew had met him in a similar tavern in Jamaica months ago, and both sides had taken an instant dislike to the other.

The two captains' eyes remained locked on each other until Umberland reached his table and sat down.

"Trouble Cap'n?" Barrel asked, seeing the expression on his face.

Silently, Captain Umberland jerked his head towards the back. "Oh God, *those* assholes," Lightning said, spotting the six men in the back booth staring at them.

"I got no use for that crew," Sam said.

"Screw 'em. We're here to celebrate!" Captain Umberland said, picking up his beer. "We're not going to let them spoil that."

"What if they decide differently?" Sam asked.

"Tankards up! Here's to being our own masters, to the sea… and to plundering!"

"To plundering!" the other three shouted as they all slammed their tankards together, banged them on the table, took long pulls, and set them back on the table in union.

"Bugger me!" Lightning suddenly exclaimed.

"Van Muis' crew?" Sam asked.

"Worse. Much worse," he responded. "Never mind them fellas; here comes *real* trouble!"

They followed his gaze and instantly spotted her.

She was five-foot-two, one-hundred pounds. She had the face of an angel, the figure of a devil, and her walk could make a priest blush.

"Savannah Hurricane, so nice to see you again," Captain Umberland said, rising out of his chair and exchanging kisses on each cheek with her.

"Mark, as I live and breathe."

"Captain Umberland."

"Of course, Mark. Whatever you say darlin'. My word, is there nowhere for a lady to sit?"

Sam and Barrel rose hurriedly, and she sat down in Barrel's seat.

"I'm going to the bar," he said. As he walked, he could feel the stares intensify from the six men in the back booth.

"So Mark, how ever have you been? Y'all been out misbehaving?"

"We've been out adventuring, yes. Rather successfully at that. How about you? Still slaying men?"

"I've never slayed a man; they simply come to me and get in over their heads."

"Oh, is that how you describe it? Sounds so... civil."

She let out a laugh and said, "Well Mark, I'm certainly not going to sit here and be judged on morality by a pirate."

"Of course not, nor will I judge. But enough of such talk. Let's get more to drink."

"I'll get it," Lightning said. "Rum or beer Captain?"

"Let's have some rum!"

"And for the lady?"

"Such manners from a pirate, I do declare. You've taught them well Mark. Whiskey darlin'."

As Lightning walked over and met Barrel at the bar, Sam turned to Savannah and said, "Where are you from again?"

She laughed and said, "Honey, my name is 'Savannah Hurricane.'"

Captain Umberland closed his eyes in embarrassment as Sam stumbled on, "Oh right, ah, I knew that. It's just, I, ah, I thought maybe you came from somewhere else."

"No darlin', born and bred in beautiful Savannah. And you Mister Sam should know that, since I've told you before."

"You have?"

"Yes indeed. The first time I met you I introduced myself as 'Savannah Hurricane, the hurricane from Savannah.'"

"Oh yeah, how could I have forgotten that?"

"One too many cannonballs to the head perhaps?"

Captain Umberland let out a laugh as Sam frowned and muttered, "I've never been hit by a cannonball."

"You never told me why you left Savannah. Too traditional?" Captain Umberland asked.

"Well they definitely tried to make me conform, and you know me Mark."

"Yeah, good luck with that."

"But really, it was the culture. Every day I would look out into the fields and see all those poor souls having to work constantly while some fat slob on a horse would shout at them to go faster. I hated slavery, still do. I just couldn't stay."

"Definitely agree with you there."

Just then Barrel and Lightning returned with the drinks.

"What took you so long?" Sam asked.

"Lightning and Lupe," Barrel responded, rolling his eyes.

"I can't help it if I'm so much more handsome than you," Lightning responded, lifting his chin up at him.

"I can fix that mate."

"That's enough from both of you," Captain Umberland said, smiling at them.

They all raised their mugs and drank. Savannah finishing hers in one go. Silence filled the table for a bit.

Then, as suddenly as she had appeared, she stood up, said, "I'm bored. Ta Mark. Boys," and walked away.

Sam opened his mouth to say something, but she was past him and gone before he could utter a word. Staring at his companions he said, "Bored? She just got here?"

"Don't try to understand that one," Barrel replied. "She's a mystery and puzzlement to all men."

"Speaking of puzzling, what's she doing over there?" Lightning said, looking over at the back booth where Savannah was sitting talking to members of the *Devil's Horn*.

"Oh shit," Captain Umberland muttered as all six suddenly stood up and marched towards them.

Sam, Barrel and Lightning immediately stood up and faced them.

"Steady lads. We're not looking for trouble," Captain Umberland said, though his right hand had moved over and was resting next to the hilt of his sword.

Captain Van Muis pushed past Sam and stood right in front of the seated Captain Umberland. "So, you think she's boring and ugly, eh Umberland!?" he said.

"Boring?" Barrel exclaimed. "*She* was the one who said she was bored."

"And no one said she was ugly." The words were still coming out of Lightning's mouth when Captain Van Muis threw a hard jab that caught Captain Umberland in the face and knocked him backwards off his chair.

Barrel responded by breaking his tankard over the head of the man closest to him. Lightning slipped past the side of the table and tackled Captain Van Muis. Sam got punched in the ribs while punching a different member of the six in the face, and in an instant, all hell broke loose.

With roars and curses from each side, the two groups furiously traded blows. Those affected by the crashing bodies and smashing furniture quickly joined in, and within a minute, a proper riot had broken out inside the tavern. Some later swore that the legendary goat itself was involved—but alas dear reader, this is a falsehood, albeit one that refuses to die.

But I digress. Inside the Crazy Goat, Captain Umberland quickly took stock of the situation. They were outnumbered, Sam was bleeding decently from the head, Barrel was busy dealing with three people, Lightning had scored some good hits but was slowing after having a chair broken over his shoulder, and finally, by sheer bad luck, most of those who had joined the fight later on had entered the fray against them.

"Barrel, Lightning, Sam; back to the ship, NOW!" Captain Umberland roared as he pushed two people over a table, clearing a path towards the door.

Even those in the town who were long accustomed to fights at the Crazy Goat were startled when 20 men came bursting out the door in rapid succession.

From inside the tavern, the voice of Savannah Hurricane was heard excitedly laughing and exclaiming, "Wheeee! That was so much fun!"

All those who had exited the tavern continued battling as they ran down the two parallel streets that led to the harbor.

"Die you bastard!" a man screamed right behind Captain Umberland.

With a lightness and quickness gained throughout years of battle, Captain Umberland completed a whirling, five-step, 360-degree turn, shooting the man dead halfway through it. Continuing on at full speed, he spotted Sam and Lightning near him, but couldn't find Barrel.

He was about to shout for him when he heard a loud crash and a death cry pierce the air from the street to his right, followed by Barrel's mocking shout: "Huzzah!"

Despite the situation, Captain Umberland couldn't help but laugh. Turning to his left, he shouted for Lightning to race ahead to the ship. Leaving the two men closest to him behind, Lightning shot forward towards the left turn that marked the start of the dock. Rounding the corner, he sprinted across the dock, shouting to the men on the *Grog Hog*.

Alerted by the massive noise coming toward them from multiple locations, Joseph and the other four were already on deck.

"Captain's in trouble! Bring up the Little Bastards!" Lightning shouted as he neared the ship. He then turned to take on the two men chasing him.

By the time they returned to the deck with three of the small portable cannons, virtually all the combatants were in the square in front of the piers where the ships were moored.

"Captain! Duck!" Joseph shouted, and then ordered the cannons to be fired from the rear of the ship.

Captain Umberland, Sam and Barrel instantly dropped to the ground as the shots whistled above them, smashing into the screaming horde behind them. Limbs were destroyed and one unlucky fellow took one right to the chest, knocking him backwards through a pile of crates.

"Great shot!" Lightning said, while battling the last of the two men who had been pursuing him.

Joseph grabbed a rifle, leaned forward, and shot the man dead.

"Even better shot!" Lightning called up to him, to which he responded with a tip of his hat.

Captain Umberland and the rest hastily climbed aboard. The other crew members followed shortly, having been alerted by all the noise. A volley of musket fire rained down on them from the *Devil's Horn*, which was moored close by. The man next to Joseph fell dead.

"Gunners to your cannons!" Captain Umberland shouted. "Jenkins, get us out of here! Get those sails up! Start pouring musket fire on those filthy dogs! MOVE!"

Across the way, similar orders were being given. Each side got off a round of cannon fire as they pulled away from the piers.

Shooters from the *Grog Hog* managed to drop a few members of the *Devil's Horn* crew, and with that, Captain Van Muis decided to call off the attack.

Both crews cursed at the other as the two ships sailed away from one another.

PAGE INTENTIONALLY LEFT BLANK

CHAPTER THREE

"That bloody harlot!" Lightning shouted once they were a safe distance away. They had stopped to sound the ship and tend to the wounded.

Pacing up and down across the deck, he ranted on. "Boring!? *She* was the one who was bored! How dare she pull a stunt like that? We could have all been killed!"

"And forget about ever going back to the Crazy Goat," Sam added gloomily.

"Yeah that too! I love that place! Now they probably won't ever let us in again."

"They'll let us back in; money rules there," Captain Umberland said, uttering his first words since he gave the order to stop.

"Can you believe that crazy wench!?" Lightning started up again.

"That's enough Lightning. We all know what she did. That's her nature. It's why she calls herself 'Hurricane.' She loves chaos."

"Captain, need to see you below when you get the chance," Jacob said, his hands and shirt stained with blood.

"Let's go now," Captain Umberland replied, following him below.

Passing the cannon deck, he paused to watch the men sluggishly attempting to repair the damage. All were either still drunk or hungover. "That bloody bitch," he muttered to himself as he looked around.

"Captain, this way please," Jacob said, gesturing further down into the ship.

As soon as the wooden door opened, the stench of death hit them like a fist. Though Captain Umberland had experienced it many times during the past three years, it still affected him.

"How bad?" he asked Jacob.

"Four dead. Two more... we'll see. The rest are hurt, but should pull through and be all right."

"Joseph," Captain Umberland said, walking quickly over to where the young man lay with his eyes shut. "How is he doing?" he asked without looking away.

"Overall, he should be all right. But..."

"But what?"

"He suffered a severe blow to the head when one of their volleys dislodged a cannon. He keeps going in and out of consciousness, and when he's awake, he seems a little... off."

"He'll pull through; he's tough."

"He should Captain, yes."

"Thank you Jacob, for everything. As always, your medical skills are invaluable to us. When you're finished down here, I need a little time with the two who are hurt badly."

"You can see them now. I've done all I can do at the moment. They are over there in the corner. I'll take my leave, with your permission."

"Yes. Thanks."

Captain Umberland walked over and spent time with each man, sharing thoughts about life and death. He thanked them for their service to the crew and congratulated them on living full lives as free men. Mostly, he urged them to keep fighting and assured them they would all feast together upon their recovery.

The next day, both men died. As they had done the day before for the four who'd perished in the battle, the entire crew gathered on deck to pay tribute.

Lightning read out the names of the two fallen pirates, and a cannon blast accompanied each one.

Then Captain Umberland stepped forward and said, "Lads, we're a family. Today we gather to remember two of our brethren who fell in defense of the ship; our home. They served well, were decent fellows and died with honor, which is a true measure of a man. We pause today to return them to the sea that they loved so. The sea upon which they roamed free from the shackles and abuses of so-called 'civilized society.'"

Placing a hand on each bundled body, he concluded, "Go now to that great hall and feast with your brothers. Know that you are not forgotten and will remain in our hearts until we all meet in the great beyond to drink together again."

Stepping aside, he watched as two crew members attached a cannonball to each body, lifted them up, and dropped them into the water below. Then each of the pirates walked forward and threw one pistol shot overboard, symbolically linking the fallen to the living.

CHAPTER FOUR

"I SAW IT! I DID!" Sam insisted excitedly.

"No you didn't. It wasn't there," Barrel replied, exasperated.

"Yes it was! I *saw* it."

"Sam, you're daft. The goat wasn't there during the fight."

"Captain I saw it during the fight! I swear!" Sam said, turning to Captain Umberland.

"He's daft Cap'n, pay him no mind," Barrel said.

"You're both daft," Captain Umberland said with a grin. Finishing his rum in one swoop, he raised his hand casually, said, "Night lads," and walked out of the tavern.

Walking down the town's main dirt road, he soon arrived at the two-story hotel that had been their home for the past week. Upon the porch that wrapped around the first floor sat First Mate Wilcox. He was sitting on a wide chair smoking a dark cigar, and offered one to Captain Umberland as he took a seat next to him.

Nodding in appreciation, he took the cigar, pulled out a small knife and cut off the cap at the end. He ran it lengthwise under his nose and inhaled deeply, savoring the strong, earthy smell that filled his nostrils. After a few more passes under his nose—a ritual that always made Wilcox smile to himself—Captain Umberland held the cigar horizontally over the candle, warming the end that was to be lit. After a few seconds, he set the cigar in his mouth and began taking quick, strong puffs while slowly rotating it in front of the flame. Bits of smoke quickly grew in size, and the tip glowed bright as he leaned back in his chair contentedly.

The two men sat in silence for a spell, smoking their cigars and drinking some of the fine local rum. The night featured typically humid, stuffy Caribbean weather, but clear skies enabled the stars to show off their brilliance.

Down the street, a well-dressed man emerged from one of the town's two brothels and made his way over to them. "Hello!" he called out to them as he reached the patio stairs. "And how are our fine traveling merchants this evening?"

"Very well Governor Tidewell," Captain Umberland replied. "And how are you Sir?"

"Excellent, thank you. I trust you and your 'employees' are enjoying your stay here?"

"Very much so. Thank you for your generous hospitality."

"You're quite welcome. Enjoy the rest of your evening gentlemen."

"You as well Governor."

They watched him continue down the street and then head off to the right, toward his large house by the water.

"How much are we paying him?" Wilcox asked.

"Enough."

Wilcox nodded and went back to puffing on his cigar.

Captain Umberland poured them both another rum. He took a sip and said, "Wilcox, are you as bored here as I am?"

Wilcox let out a small laugh, "Yes Captain."

"It's just that there's not much to do. A few pubs, a few brothels, but nothing like the excitement and energy of the normal spots."

"True, it is pretty dull. Though it's an ideal place for the wounded to recover, and keeps the rest of the crew from getting into trouble."

"Very true."

Wilcox looked over at Umberland and could tell the moment had come. "Suppose it's about time to be moving on, eh?"

"It's time."

"What's next Captain? Where are we heading from here?"

Captain Umberland took a long pull from his cigar and the accompanying smoke partially obscured his face for a moment. When it cleared, Wilcox saw that he was looking intently at the buildings across from them. He took two more long pulls, producing a great amount of smoke, and finished the rest of his rum in one go, throwing his head back in the process.

Setting his cup roughly back on the small table between them, he looked at Wilcox and said, "We're going to head southwest to Panama and hit the city of Rojanz. It's not too large, yet houses a decent amount of the Spanish king's gold. Before we make for Rojanz, we'll purchase a vessel and use it for supplies and extra gunpowder, shot and cannonballs."

Wilcox nodded and said, "Sounds like a good plan. Another ship would certainly help. How do you know this town has gold there?"

"Captain Low raided it some months back. I heard him talking about it in a pub the last time we were in Kingston."

"Low? Don't have no use for that one. He's a butcher, not a pirate."

"No argument here. Know how he found out about the gold at Rojanz? He had captured a ship off the Panamanian coast and was interrogating the captives. He asked one man where he was from and the man replied, 'Rojanz.' Low asked him what was there, and the man trembled and didn't respond. So Low employed what he calls his 'favorite little game.' He wrapped thin rope around the man's fingers and then twice over the top of the knuckles. Then he lit the rope."

"Damn. What happened?"

"The man immediately told Low that Rojanz was one of the Spanish king's smaller treasury towns, and a decent amount of gold was stored there."

"I see... what happened to the man?"

"Low refused to extinguish the rope, and the fire burned the man's fingers down to the bones. Then he had the screaming man thrown overboard."

"Into the saltwater? What a way to go."

"Low's heartless. But anyway, they must have replenished Rojanz's gold by now. Should be a good score."

"It'll be better defended this time."

"The defenses will certainly be strengthened somewhat, but you can't stay fully alert forever. We'll have surprise and determination on our side. When we get close to Rojanz, we'll wait out in deep water while you and a few of the lads row ashore close to the town. Then you can view the defenses at night and return to us before dawn. From there, we'll plot our final attack strategy."

"Sounds good Captain. When do you want to leave?"

"Let's stay here for another two days. That'll give the wounded a bit more time to rest up and will allow me to dine with Governor Tidewell one more time."

"Very good. I'll inform the men tomorrow."

"Just tell them that we're leaving in two days. I'll explain the specifics to them at the feast tomorrow night."

"Aye Captain."

With that, the conversation ceased for a bit as they turned their attention to fresh cigars and rum.

The Royal Inn was the closest thing the small island had to a fancy location. It was a one-story structure that served as the meeting place of the "well-to-do" crowd, as well as where they entertained any visiting merchants of note. Tonight it was reserved solely for Captain Umberland and his 50-strong crew.

The room was fully illuminated by tall candleholders that held five candles each and lined the room. There was a massive 12-candle chandelier handing from the center of the ceiling as well.

"So what's next Captain?" Sam asked as they feasted on roasted chicken with onions and sweet peppers, dark bread, potatoes and various cakes. "Wilcox said that we're leaving the day after tomorrow. Don't get me wrong; it'll be good to go. Kinda quiet around here. But what's the plan?"

Everyone stopped eating and turned their attention to the captain.

"Sam my boy, I'm glad you asked. Lads, we're about to set off on our most ambitious adventure yet! Nothing we've done so far compares to this, and it's going to take everything we've got to pull it off."

Captain Umberland set down his drink and leaned in, the intensity of both his eyes and his voice increasing. He set both hands on the table, palms down with his fingers spread out, as if he was gripping it with all his might, and said, "What we're about to undertake will be full of danger, cunning, risk and boldness. But if we succeed, we will acquire a most spectacular prize!"

The men all shouted in support, with several of them banging their tankards on the table.

"What's the prize Captain?" Lightning asked, shouting above the noise.

The smile on Captain Umberland's face grew as he looked around and said, "We're going to hit the town of Rojanz on the Panamanian coast! It's got gold, jewels and other valuables that the Spanish have been plundering from the native population. Now it's decently defended lads, but with the proper combination of cunning and preparation, it'll be ours!"

Even more shouts, cheers and pounding on the table broke out as the men envisioned the prize.

"How are we going to take it Cap'n?" Barrel asked.

"Yeah Captain, how are we going to take it?" Parrot chimed in.

"This town has been struck before, so it'll be decently defended. We're going to acquire a ship before we leave here and convert it into a supply vessel. Wilcox will captain it. When we're close, he will take a few of you ashore to scout the defenses. Upon their return, we'll determine the best plan of attack, hit them, and take the town!"

"And the gold!" Lightning shouted.

"And the jewels!" Sam added.

"We'll take it all!" Captain Umberland roared.

"Three cheers for the Cap'n!" Barrel hollered.

All the men rose and shouted "Huzzah!" three times in unison.

Deep into the night the candles burned bright, the celebratory sounds rising as drinks, food and companionship raged on. The darkened sky was losing its daily battle with the dawn when the last of the pirates stumbled out, and the candles were finally extinguished.

Part 2: Estevez

PAGE INTENTIONALLY LEFT BLANK

CHAPTER FIVE

THE WIND WAS BLOWING over the island of New Seville as the pirate ship *Buena Vista* sailed into its harbor. Stepping onto the pier, Captain Eduardo Martinez Javier Estevez presented an impressive figure. He was 6'6", 250 pounds with a muscular frame, flowing jet-black hair, and a neatly-trimmed goatee. He was only 20 years old; however, life experience and years at sea had matured him rapidly. Calling out for his First Mate Sausalito Sanchez to follow him, he headed across the dock and up the street. As he went, he couldn't help but notice the construction work that was taking place around the dock. Pausing, he inquired what had happened; the bullet holes and cannonball damage made it clear that this wasn't a normal upgrade.

"A bunch of people fought out here yesterday," a dock worker informed him.

Nodding, he thanked the man for the information and continued on.

Arriving at the Crazy Goat, he was a bit startled to see the interior smashed up.

"Genarrio! How are you? Are you all right?" he asked the proprietor upon spotting him by the bar.

"Who's that? Ah, Captain Estevez. Finally a civilized man. How are you my friend? Sausalito, good to see you again."

Shaking both men's hands, he led them over to the bar and insisted on buying their first round. Estevez ordered tequila, while Sausalito got a tankard of beer. Genarrio was already drinking whiskey.

"Thank you for your hospitality Genarrio. Now tell us what happened here. A man at the dock said something about two groups of people fighting each other?"

"Yes, last night. Two pirate crews were drinking here and then suddenly things went nuts. The place got wrecked, and they headed down to the docks still fighting. I heard cannon fire near the end. Crazy night my friend."

"Pirate crews were fighting each other eh? A bit unusual, but definitely not unheard of; we have been known to be a bit rambunctious from time to time."

Genarrio tried to laugh, but his heart wasn't in it.

Setting his drink down, Estevez patted him on the shoulder, the weariness evident in his eyes.

"Interestingly enough, it's actually a fellow pirate who brings us here today. I wonder if he was involved in this. Do you know the names of the captains who were fighting?"

"Umberland and that Dutch guy... Van-something."

"Umberland! Umberland!! He's the one I'm looking for! Is he still on the island!? Is he here!?"

Startled, Genarrio stammered, "I'm, uh, I'm not sure. There was all the commotion here... then the cannon fire down at the docks. All I know is that neither crew came back here."

"Sausalito, *Störtebeker!*"

Both men grabbed their drinks and downed them in one go.

Grabbing Genarrio's shoulder, he thanked him vigorously for the information and said that if he saw or heard about Umberland again, to please send word to the pub called the Red Cape on the island of Borracho. With that, he turned and bolted for the door.

"Captain! Wait!" Genarrio called out.

"What is it!?"

Hurrying over to the door, he looked around and then motioned for the two men to follow him outside.

"I'm sorry *Señor*, but we're in a terrible rush," Estevez said, his eyes already looking down the road towards the dock.

"I know I know! But this is important. There was somebody here a few days ago looking for *you*."

Returning his gaze to Genarrio, Estevez leaned forward and said in a lower voice, "Who was looking for me?"

"I don't know his name; he didn't say. I've never seen the fellow before. I didn't like him. Seemed like he was up to no good. He was very interested in you though. Kept asking if I knew you, then was asking patrons if they had any idea where you might be."

"Describe him."

"From his accent, I would say he was from southern Spain. Medium-height, thin, dark hair, ummm, scar across his forehead."

"Anything else?"

"*Si*, he gave me a gold piece and promised 50 more if I gave him information that led to him finding you. Very bad my friend. Be careful, I don't like this."

"Nor do I. However I'm extremely grateful for the heads up. You're one of the best of them Genarrio. Please send word to me at the Red Cape if this man returns, or if you hear anything more about him."

"I will Captain. Until next time my friend."

The two embraced, and then Estevez and Sausalito rushed down to the dock to seek information about Umberland.

No one there was able to tell him where Umberland had headed, but they did confirm that neither he nor Van Muis were still on the island.

After obtaining a rough heading for Umberland's ship, Estevez rounded up the members of his crew who were in local pubs and immediately left the island in pursuit.

CHAPTER SIX

CAPTAIN ESTEVEZ PACED the around the bow of the ship frustrated. It had been 10 days, yet there was no sign of Captain Umberland either on the water or in the towns where they had inquired after him. Estevez kept staring sideways at the water while he walked, as if willing the ship to appear.

"Anything Captain?" Plato said, approaching Estevez by the bow.

"Nothing. Same as the day before, and the day before that. Damn!" Estevez said, punching the mast hard. Balling his fingers into a fist and then loosening them, his knuckles habitually red, he went back to pacing.

"Such is life. Sometimes the harder you reach for something, the further it recedes from your grasp."

"I know. Not in the mood for your life observations right now. I want Umberland. I want to make him pay for what he did!"

"I understand. Would you like some time alone?"

"I don't want anything except to find Umberland."

"We will."

"Plato, I need a few minutes alone with the Captain," Sausalito said, approaching them.

After Plato left, Sausalito leaned against the mast and said, "We're getting low on supplies."

"I know."

"I know you want to find Umberland, we all do, but the supply situation cannot be ignored any longer."

"We'll pick up more in the next town we stop in."

"About that... we're also running short on money."

For a minute neither spoke. Suddenly, one of those rare moments in life occurred when the exact thing they needed appeared at the exact moment they needed it.

"Sails! Starboard side!" Javier called out from up in the Crow's Nest.

Estevez shot Sausalito a wicked smile.

"You lucky bastard," was all Sausalito replied.

"All hands on deck! Everyone, to your positions! Hoist the colors!" Estevez shouted as he ran across the deck.

The crew rushed into their positions as the black flag was raised to the top of the mast. In the middle of the flag was a red skeleton holding a large cutlass with both hands. A full moon was in the upper left corner, while an 8-spoke sailing wheel was in the upper right corner. The skeleton stood for the crew's bravery. The full moon signified that they were free from society's constraints. The wheel represented that they were masters of their lives.

As the distance between them narrowed, Estevez saw that there were actually two ships ahead. The ship on the right was the larger of the two and he decided to attack it first, as he figured they wouldn't expect it.

Like a horse starting to gallop, the ship surged forward aided by a fortuitous wind. Nearing the larger vessel, the *Buena Vista* was starting to move into position when the vessel suddenly turned and several cannons on deck were aimed in their direction.

"Hard to port!" Estevez yelled to the helmsman, Hierro Manos.

The *Buena Vista* quickly veered away, and Estevez ordered it to target the smaller vessel.

The smaller vessel turned in an attempted to get alongside the larger one, but the *Buena Vista* maneuvered between them, which also prevented the larger ship from firing its cannons at them for fear of hitting their sister ship.

"Move fast!" Estevez shouted. "We have to take them before the larger ship can get in position to help!"

Getting alongside the smaller ship, the pirates fixed hooks and raced aboard, while others aboard the *Buena Vista* poured cover fire down at the defenders. Screaming at the top of their lungs, the pirates surged across the smaller ship's deck and decimated those who were foolish enough to pull iron and face them. Witnessing the pirates drop the last of those facing them, the rest of the passengers and crew promptly surrendered.

Captain Estevez ordered all those who had surrendered to move over to the bow of the *Buena Vista* and had them stand against the railing, facing the approaching larger vessel. He put Javier in command of a four-person crew aboard the now-empty smaller vessel and then ordered the two ships to separate. Standing in the middle of the deck, he ordered the *Buena Vista* to sail right at the larger ship.

Onboard the larger ship, the captain looked out helplessly at his imprisoned friends standing against the railing facing him. He knew he couldn't fire on the pirate vessel and realized that further resistance would only result in the deaths of those already imprisoned, if not all of them. This was confirmed when the pirate ship arrived and Captain Estevez vowed that they would kill one prisoner for every shot fired at them.

Bowing to the inevitable, the captain of the larger ship capitulated without a fight, imploring Estevez to stick to his word and not harm any of the prisoners if the larger ship surrendered immediately.

The haul from the two ships was impressive; gold and silver coins, along with plenty of precious jewels, were promptly moved into the *Buena Vista's* hold. A healthy amount of wine and rum was also secured. Taking the larger ship as a prize, the pirates marooned the crew and passengers on a nearby island. Though it was deserted, they knew it was near the shipping lanes and would only be a few days at most before someone spotted them. They left those stranded enough food and wine for three days; four if they rationed properly.

Using the smaller ship as target practice, Estevez had his gunners get in some live fire practice and they promptly sunk it. Nodding satisfactorily, he ordered Hierro to sail for the island of Santa Muerte.

CHAPTER SEVEN

THE ISLAND OF SANTA Muerte was named after the female Spanish Angel of Death. The harbor entrance was protected by an old royal fort that had been abandoned long ago when the Spanish moved to a larger facility on a more southerly island.

To further protect the harbor, the pirates who took over the location years ago procured the services of the mad architect Sherman, who installed his famous Sherman's Jaw in it.

Sherman hailed from Wales but had moved to London to study architecture. Upon graduating he found employment at one of the city's premier firms. After years of being passed over for a promotion in favor of less-talented English architects, he brought the issue up with his boss, asking what he could do to be of additional value to them. For his "impertinence," he was promptly sacked. His former employer then falsely accused him of stealing his co-workers' designs, thus guaranteeing no other architectural firm would consider hiring him. His reputation shattered, he found solace in the intoxicating stimulants being brought in from the New World. He quickly discovered he had a remarkable capacity for them and could consume far more than the average person. Word quickly spread about his extremely erratic behavior, and his already damaged reputation was irreparably destroyed. His finances failing, he decided to head to the Caribbean to put his talents to use for the pirates who were so loathed in England. On the voyage across the Atlantic, he vowed to do everything he could to thwart the Crown's fight against pirates and bring misery to warships of any nation that attacked them.

To that end he created his Sherman's Jaw, which was a device strung across the bottom of a harbor's entrance and operated by reinforced pulleys hidden on either side. Lying flat on the bottom were a series of heavy iron spikes welded to a thick iron base. If an enemy ship attempted to enter the harbor, the spikes could be raised to deliver a lethal blow. Even if a ship was strong enough to survive the impact and continue sailing to the pier, the damage inflicted either caused it to sink or forced most of the crew to stay behind and frantically work to keep it afloat, thus severely reducing the attacker's strength.

When first deployed, the device greatly surprised the English. Two ships were totally lost, while a few others were severely damaged but managed to limp away. Shortly after, the English ceased sailing into pirate harbors. This greatly increased the device's demand among scallywag strongholds and business boomed for Sherman. However the rise in revenue and workload only increased his active consumption of stimulants.

The sun was low in the sky when the *Buena Vista* tied up at the pier and the crew poured out onto the dock. Santa Muerte was one of Estevez' favorite haunts and he smiled upon setting foot on her shores. He gave the crew a week's leave to do as they pleased with their share of the treasure. He didn't want to wait, but he could sense the crew's desire to celebrate. They had done well during the assault on the ships and deserved to unwind; better drunk than bitter. He also wanted to speak alone with Sausalito regarding the news Genarrio had shared with them.

The two of them needed a quiet pub to talk about serious matters, but first there was a stop to be made. Joining several crew members who animatedly walked along the many bars and whorehouses lining the dock, they all arrived at the same destination: *El Rojo Guadaña*, the Red Scythe.

The pub was always lively and known for the quality of both the women employed there and the musical entertainment. Upon entering the front door, one found the bar to the left against the back wall. The table and chairs filled the large, open room. The wall on the other side facing the bar was curved and musicians occupied small stages on both the far right and left side of it. Above the bar was the true attraction however; a balcony big enough for two had been installed. On it the two house musicians played "Dueling Guitars" all night long. Few better guitarists could be found, and they were known throughout all pirate haunts.

The pub was run by a husband and wife duo from Seville. Hailing from the home of some of the best guitar music in the world, they insisted on music being a key feature. The husband was named Raul and he oversaw the drinks. The wife was named Raven and she organized the pub's female companions. Together they handled the finances. Like the musicians, their reputation was known far and wide.

Raul's face lit up upon seeing Captain Estevez walk through the door. He hurried over, joyfully greeted each crew member, and gave Estevez a large hug.

"My friend, great to see you! When did you get in?"

"Raul, you know we would never go anywhere before heading here!"

"Captain, tell 'em about the ships we just took!" said Tornado.

"I'm sure he's busy with other things. Another time."

"No no, please, tell me about your latest adventure!"

Captain Estevez told the tale about the capture of the two ships that had just taken place, with Tornado excitedly interjecting exaggerated elements, and Javier nodding solemnly when the part about him taking command of the smaller ship was mentioned.

The smile on Raul's face grew as the story unfolded, and he slapped Estevez on the back heartily upon its completion. "Well done! Well done to all of you! Brilliant tactics!"

"I'm not sure how brilliant it was, but it worked!" Estevez responded.

Calling out to the nearby bartender to give the crew members a free first round, he procured a bottle of wine and gestured for Estevez to follow him to small back courtyard that was reserved for the owners and whomever they chose to accompany them.

Sitting down, Raul filled two glasses with wine and they both said, "*Salud.*"

After taking a sip, the smile disappeared from his face. He looked right at Estevez and said, "Unfortunately I have some very serious news to share with you my friend."

"Someone recently visited you and inquired about my location? Someone willing to pay handsomely for the information?"

Raul's eyes opened wide and he said, "How did you... you dog!"

Estevez smiled mischievously as Raul continued, "Be careful out there; the man was very interested in you."

"So it seems. Did he happen to mention his name?"

"No, nor did he say why he was seeking you."

"Of course. It was the same in the other location."

"Where else did you hear the news?"

"Genarrio told me, at the Crazy Goat in New Seville."

"Don't know the man personally, but New Seville is a decent place."

Both men finished their wine and Estevez poured fresh glasses. As he was finishing, Raul reached into his pocket and pulled out a robed female figure holding a globe. Extending his arm, he said, "I got this for you."

Taking the figure Estevez replied, "Thank you... what is it?"

"*Nuestra Señora de la Santa Muerte.*"

"Our Lady of the Holy Death?"

"Correct. She is a protector, and of course, our island's namesake. I chose this one because of the globe. May her protection extend to you no matter where you sail. Evil abounds in this uncertain world of ours. May her protective robes keep you safe against this man who hunts you."

"Thank you my friend; I shall treasure it."

Upon finishing their second glasses of wine, the two hugged goodbye and Estevez went to find Sausalito.

Finding him at a table with Tornado, Javier, Plato, Hierro Manos and a few others, he sat with them for one glass of wine. Despite their protests, he insisted that he and Sausalito had something to discuss in private and the two bade the group goodnight.

Heading away from the popular dock area, they made their way deeper into town. The rubbish piling up in the streets and the boarded-up windows informed them that they had arrived in a section where no one was likely to know them.

Halfway down a side street, they found a small building with no windows and a faded sign that read: The Rotting Oar. Drinks.

The pub was dull and dimly-lit. A few old tables and chairs were spread out across the room. The bar was on the right side and contained half the bottles that a normal pub did. Three people were spread out around the room, drinking quietly. A couple more were at the bar, talking dejectedly to the bartender.

Ordering a bottle of red wine, Estevez and Sausalito sat down at a table in the back. They adjusted their chairs so both could see the pub's only door.

Silently, one of them filled both of the ceramic beakers. They raised them up, said "*Salud,*" and took a sip. They had both poured a second cup before either of them uttered a word.

"You realize that if it's his family that's hunting you, they won't give up until they find you," Sausalito said.

"Find *us.*"

"They won't stop until they kill you."

"Kill *us.*"

"Thanks. That's helping."

Captain Estevez grinned at Sausalito until his first mate finally shook his head and let out a small laugh.

"That's it!?" Captain Estevez said in mock horror. "We're wanted men! Shaking our fists at death itself, and the best you can do is let out that pitiful excuse for a laugh!? A powerful individual is determined to kill us! We'll soon face her mercenaries who appear dedicated solely to sending us down to dine with Old Roger! Surely that must get your blood flowing!"

"Oh sure Captain, I love it."

"*Mierda!* What am I going to do with you?"

Sausalito shrugged his shoulders.

Captain Estevez downed his wine in one gulp and poured himself another beaker. Holding the bottle up at an angle, he returned it to the table and said, "We're going to need more soon."

"Always. I'll get it."

Returning with another bottle, Sausalito poured the last of the wine from the first bottle into his beaker. They clinked beakers, said "*Salud,*" and drank.

Both tensed and cast hard looks at the door as it opened, and a man wandered in. Watching him cross over to the bar and take a seat, they didn't take their eyes off him until he had ordered and was drinking his beer.

Relaxing slightly, they both looked at each other.

"Crazy bitch," Captain Estevez finally said.

"Crazy like her brother."

"Her brother was worse, but greed was his sin. She's definitely the more vengeful one."

"Her brother getting killed probably had something to do with that."

"He had it coming. More than had it coming."

"Damn right. Straight scum. Despicable person."

"Despicable… and heartless. *Heartless.*"

Both men silently drank their wine for a bit, each engrossed in their own thoughts.

"You really think it's her?" Sausalito said upon completing yet another beaker.

"It has to be; no one else would search for us so thoroughly. For us specifically."

"Yeah, suppose so. It's been a year you know? A year since we took to pirating."

"A year since I killed her brother."

"And used the money we plundered from his house to purchase the *Buena Vista*."

"He was just a petty noble."

"Petty or not, he was still a noble."

"He stole my father's land."

"I know. He was scum… but he was noble scum."

"My father was a great winemaker. Oh, he wasn't rich by any means, but he made damn good wine. Just wasn't that great at promoting it."

"I only had it a few times when I was younger, but I always enjoyed it."

The wine was starting to get a hold of Captain Estevez as they dove into the third bottle. Holding up his beaker, he allowed the wine to transport himself back to the small village in southern Spain that he originally hailed from.

"My father loved his vineyards. He loved the process of making wine, the tradition of it, the life of it. He was so alive back in those old days. He loved the earth that his grapes grew in almost as much as he loved my mother."

Sausalito nodded in agreement, the redness in his cheeks increasing with each passing drink.

"My father was connected to the earth in a way that people from the city will never understand. And then one day, it was all taken from him. One day, that bastard Don Ladrón swooped in and took it! *Stole* my father's land. He who already had everything; no, that wasn't enough! He cast his gaze on our little parcel, and just had to have it!"

The hatred flashed across Captain Estevez' eyes and he stared at the wall with a look that would make lions tremble in their dens.

"Drove your father into an early grave sadly," Sausalito said solemnly. He knew the story well, having been Estevez' best friend growing up.

"It truly did. He had to accept a job in town at some horrible business, doing the most soulless, mind-numbing work imaginable. He hated that job so much; he used to come home so pained by it. So pained at having been torn from his vines."

"He got swindled, no doubt about that. And no one would stand up to a noble of course."

"Of course not. The only one who stood by me during those horrible years after, was you."

"Always *amigo*."

The two smiled at one another and clinked beakers.

"It made me sad to leave you, but after watching my father suffer for four years after losing his land, I couldn't take it anymore. As soon as I turned 16, I was gone. Took two trips to the New World, each time sailing under a captain more sadistic than any criminal out there. How they loved the lash, those tiny tyrants."

"A great many men wouldn't turn to piracy if the 'honest' captains weren't so horrible."

"That was my experience, for sure. I had just returned to Spain after the second voyage when word reached me that my father had died. I visited Mom, paid my respects at his grave, and that very night, determined that I would never share his fate. I remember it clearly; I was drinking in one of those beautiful cellar cantinas, with the exposed brick and soft candlelight. The ones where the music bounces around the walls and the laughter flows as freely as the wine. I love them so. I was watching the owner serving drinks with a smile and chatting with the regulars, and he seemed so happy. What I realized in that moment was that I was just as trapped as my father had been. For all my talk, I hadn't escaped anything. Sure I was at sea, but I was under the command of despicable captains who made my life miserable every day. So I decided right then to become a pirate, to be totally free! I vowed to live a full life, rich with experiences, master of my fate, owing nothing to anyone. I pledged that I would never end up trapped, as my father had been. I vowed this for both of us. So now I'm living the life he didn't get to live. In a sense, I'm living the life that was taken from him. While he may be gone, I keep him with me in my heart at all times. He lives on through my exploits."

"I heard your mother's situation improved as well," Sausalito said with a roguish smile.

Estevez leaned back in his chair, cocked his head to one side, and smilingly said, "If enough money to support her and my two sisters magically appeared on her doorstep one day, that's nothing I'd know anything about."

Both laughed heartily and clinked beakers with the gusto that accompanies increased consumption of alcohol.

"Ahhh Sausalito, what a year it has been since that night! The first thing I did was enlist the aid of you, my best friend in the world, and together we took to the seas as the finest pirates out there!"

"Well first we took vengeance on the noble who stole your father's land, and then robbed his house, and then got the ship."

"Yes we did. Finally, my father can truly rest in peace."

"That is a wonderful thing for sure, but apparently the past is coming back to haunt us."

"I wonder how she found out it was me who killed her brother."

"Process of elimination I'd imagine. They're not going to let the robbery and murder of a noble go unsolved. You must have been near the top of the list of suspects. And once they heard about some of our early exploits, I'm sure they figured it out."

"True," Captain Estevez said, before gesturing for Sausalito to lean in closer. "Listen my friend, we both know that the person hunting us can't be reasoned with. We have to destroy him."

"And then...?"

"Then we'll have to sail back to the Old Country and deal with the sister. She's as heartless as the summer sun is merciless."

"Agreed. We shouldn't tell the crew this yet. Let's deal with the person hunting us first."

"Absolutely."

"How do we find him?"

"No clue. We've been heading southwest and at both places we've stopped, the locals have said the man was already there. Let's keep going in that heading and see if we can catch up and surprise him."

"What about Umberland?"

The anger flashed in Estevez's eyes again. Setting down his wine he said, "We will deal with him in due time. Unfortunately, that'll have to wait, but he will pay for what he did!"

Sausalito nodded in agreement and proceeded to pour the last of the bottle.

Looking around, Estevez said, "Let's get the hell outta here."

"Back to *El Rojo Guadaña*?"

Estevez nodded. The two of them downed the remaining wine and headed out.

PAGE INTENTIONALLY LEFT BLANK

Part 3:
Montpellier

PAGE INTENTIONALLY LEFT BLANK

CHAPTER EIGHT

A BREEZE WAS BLOWING across the town of Santa Fermin, providing a welcome relief to the ever-present humidity. Dock hands reached out and grabbed the lines thrown to them by the vessel that had just maneuvered into position. A four-man guard exited and waited for the official to disembark.

Marching two in front and two behind, the five men made their way into town. A short walk brought them to the Treasury House.

"May I help you *Señor*?" the clerk stammered, looking up with a start at the official in front of him.

The official handed the man a document featuring the Royal Seal and replied curtly, "I've been ordered to ship the treasury here back to His Majesty Charles II. Procure it immediately. We depart in one hour."

Reading the paper, the man stiffened, saluted the official and said, "*Si Señor*, right away!" He then ordered the island's eight chests of gold and silver coins to be brought up.

As the official and his 4-man guard waited, the island's governor appeared. Looking at the official he said, "I am Governor Alvarez. No one informed me that you were to arrive. What is your purpose *Señor*?"

The official nodded and replied, "My name is *Señor* Vampa. I have been ordered by His Majesty Charles II to bring the royal treasure located on this island back to Spain."

"His Majesty Charles II is five years old."

"Pardon me. I meant his mother, the Queen Regent Mariana, has ordered me to bring the treasure back to Spain. It is desperately needed, as the country is in danger of bankruptcy."

"I am aware. The country has faced bankruptcy in the past, but never before has the King or the Queen Regent asked for our entire treasury to be transferred at once."

"You choose to question the decision of the Queen Regent?"

"Of course not *Señor* Vampa. Please excuse the comment." Turning to the clerk, he asked to see the document. After reviewing it, he nodded and returned it to the clerk.

"Everything looks in order *Señor*. The chests should arrive promptly. I'll go check on the progress. Excuse me."

With a nod, Governor Alvarez exited the room. The official looked at the clerk, who was sitting silently behind his desk. He seemed nervous from the back-and-forth conversation that had just taken place.

The official ordered two of the four guards to stand watch outside.

"How many chests are there total?" he asked the clerk.

"I'm, uh, I'm not sure *Señor.*"

The official gave the man a hard look, and the room fell silent again.

The clerk was shuffling some papers on his desk when a voice shouting in French caused him to look up suddenly. Stunned, he watched as *"Señor* Vampa" and the two guards rushed out of the building and started yelling in French at the other two guards.

Running to the window, he looked out and saw Governor Alvarez leading a contingent of 20 soldiers towards the five men standing outside.

"Captain, what do we do!?" Coqauvin said over his shoulder as they faced the approaching contingent of soldiers. "We're cut off from the boat!"

"Follow me *copains!*" Captain Montpellier yelled as he bolted to the left and ran past the Treasury House with the other four right behind him.

The 20 soldiers took off in pursuit with Governor Alvarez in front screaming, "Death to pirates! No Quarter!"

The five pirates raced across a small square as musket fire was directed at them from more soldiers in one of the buildings.

Townspeople screamed and scrambled out of the way as they thundered down the road, the roar of the pursuing soldiers behind them.

In the distance, multiple muffled booms reverberated from the island.

"We're firing our cannons at them!" Rhodes shouted with a smile on his face.

"No we're not; *they* are firing at our ship," Sampson said dejectedly, as the group ducked more musket fire directed at them.

"Shit!" Captain Montpellier shouted as they rounded a corner and saw 10 additional soldiers in front of them preparing to fire. "This way!"

The five jumped a small stone wall and shouldered open the back door of a house. The wife screamed and the husband cursed as the pirates flew through the house. The wife screamed again as 20 soldiers and the governor arrived a few seconds later and thundered past. The husband frantically gestured in the direction they'd gone.

Emerging from the house, Captain Montpellier led the men through backyards and front yards heading towards the water, with bullets whizzing past them continuously. Nimbler and with greater experience in fast-moving battle scenarios, the pirates managed to increase their lead.

The sound of the island's cannons firing at the pirate ship had been joined by the equally loud sound of the pirates firing back. Onboard the ship, First Mate Charles Fontaine shouted at the helmsman, "Luc, hard to port!"

The pirates had already cut away the lines tying them to the dock once the shooting had begun. The large ship, disguised as a Spanish royal naval vessel, turned and headed left, sailing parallel to the coast. Fontaine could hear the musket fire getting louder as they approached the middle of the island. The ship had taken a few rounds from the shore cannons, but no major damage had been sustained.

Slightly ahead of them, five men burst out of the trees and onto the beach.

"Captain!" Fontaine shouted to one of the men on the beach, and then quickly gave the order to lower the anchor.

"Fontaine! Look ahead! There on the beach!" one of the men on the deck shouted to him, pointing to his right.

"Shit!" Fontaine uttered, looking at the 10 new soldiers who had emerged further up the beach and were running towards the five pirates stuck on the island.

"Keep sailing! Hit them with the cannons!" Captain Montpellier shouted as he and the other four started to run towards the advancing 10 soldiers.

Behind them, the sounds of the soldiers who had been pursuing them grew to a roar as they rushed through the trees and onto the beach.

"Captain! Behind you!" Fontaine shouted from the Quarterdeck.

Montpellier continued running towards the soldiers in front of him, who had stopped, dropped to one knee, and were preparing to fire.

"Starboard battery! FIRE!" came the command from Fontaine.

The ship's right side cannons thundered to life and decimated the soldiers on the beach who were preparing to fire.

"Throw the anchor!" Fontaine yelled. "Gunners to the stern, NOW! Lay down covering fire for the captain! Ready two boats! Get over to that beach!"

The gunners rushed to the back of the ship and began firing the small rear cannons at the soldiers and the island's governor, who took cover in the trees. From there, the soldiers continued to fire at the five pirates who had situated themselves behind a row of palm trees at the edge of the beach.

Six men each jumped into the two small boats that had been lowered into the water and rowed across to the island. The gunners continued to fire on the area that the group of soldiers had taken cover in, preventing them from advancing on Montpellier and the other four.

As soon as the two small boats reached the beach, Fontaine ordered a fresh round of cannon fire. Montpellier and the four pirates sprinted across the beach to the waiting boats. Under the protection provided by the ship's cannons, they quickly made it back to the ship and were hauled aboard.

"Captain! Head for open water?" Luc shouted from the helm.

"No! Turn us around immediately. Take us back to the dock!"

"Captain?"

"Are you crazy!?" Fontaine shouted, staring at him wide-eyed. "We're all lucky to be alive! The ruse didn't work! We need to get the hell out of here now!"

Captain Montpellier threw Fontaine a devious smile and repeated the command to head back to the dock. Then he ordered the crew into position.

"Captain," Fontaine started to say before being immediately interrupted by Montpellier.

"Cousin, I've heard your objections and understand your concerns. However in life, one must be bold! That is whom fortune favors. And now is a time for boldness!"

"Fortune indeed favors the bold. But this isn't boldness; it's madness! You'll send us all down to the bottom to dine with Old Roger!"

"One way to find out!"

The ship completed its turn and fired a full cannon volley from the port battery as it took off back towards the main dock.

The ship's crew was silent as they sailed parallel to the island, following its gentle curve to the left.

"So what's the plan?" Fontaine asked, the nervousness evident in his voice.

"Well, I figure that virtually every soldier they have on the island is either back there where they were shooting at us or running towards the area. So guess what's unprotected for a short while until they all return?"

"I'll be damned!"

"Whom does fortune favor cousin?"

Fontaine shook his head and laughingly said, "You."

"Exactly!"

"How do you want to attack any soldiers who may have been left behind?"

"Go straight at 'em! Show no mercy!"

"Captain, we're almost there," Luc called out as the dock appeared in front of them.

Only one of the shore cannons fired at them as they docked. The pirates raced down the pier, screaming as loudly as possible. The two soldiers who had remained and were manning the lone cannon looked upon the approaching pirates like the Romans must have viewed the attacking Visigoths when Rome fell over a thousand years earlier.

The pirates made quick work of the soldiers and then headed unopposed to the Treasury House. Smashing through the door, they grabbed the terrified clerk and threatened him with a most unspeakable punishment if he didn't immediately tell them where the chests of gold were kept.

Following his directions, several pirates ran deeper into the structure and down into the basement. Struggling back up the stairs, they had retrieved four chests when Montpellier yelled at them to bring what they had immediately and get back to the ship.

The pirates could hear the sounds of the returning soldiers growing ever louder and ever closer as they struggled to carry the chests.

Montpellier ran ahead and yelled for more crew and more muskets to come forward. 25 pirates raced down the pier to join him, and together they formed a defensive line at the end of the pier.

The first of the island's soldiers to make it back to the area were greeted with a round of musket fire. They immediately turned and took cover behind the building they had just passed.

Montpellier implored the pirates carrying the treasure to move faster, while yelling commands to the pirates protecting them.

More soldiers arrived and began firing at the pirates. Montpellier ordered one last volley to be fired at them as the ones carrying the treasure finally reached him. Moving aside to let them down the pier first, he and the other 25 quickly followed.

The soldiers raced to try and stop them, but, having already fired their one-shot muskets and being severely restricted in movement due to the narrowness of the pier, they stood no chance. The rear guard of the pirates battled sword-to-sword with them between running down the pier towards the ship.

Once they got close enough, the pirates on the ship were able to provide covering fire. The soldiers continued forward bravely and a few of them were felled by the sharpshooters. Slowed by the shots and now vastly outmanned, they paused to reload. The pirates cut the holding lines and sailed away, leaving the soldiers to fire a few futile rounds at them in frustration.

PAGE INTENTIONALLY LEFT BLANK

CHAPTER NINE

24 HOURS AFTER SUCCESSFULLY plundering the four chests of gold and silver from the Spanish island, Captain Montpellier and the crew of the ship *Cheval* were on their way to the legendary pirate island of Borracho. Excitement abounded onboard, and all were in good spirits.

Standing by the bow, Captain Montpellier and First Mate Fontaine were each consuming a bottle of wine and jovially recounting the previous day's adventure.

"You should have seen the clerk's face Fontaine! He looked confused, worried and scared all at once."

"He must have been completely stunned!"

"Oh he was!" Montpellier said before growing quiet. "It was going so well Fontaine, until that bastard governor showed up. Totally ruined everything. I tell you, the clerk was falling for it up until that point."

"Shame. All that time spent copying the Royal Seal from the document we found on that Spanish ship we captured a few months ago."

"I know. It was a beautiful piece of forgery. Oh well, at least we still made off with four chests of gold!"

Both men burst out laughing and drank again.

"Captain! Port side; look!" Sampson shouted down from the Crow's Nest.

Both men jumped slightly at the agitated voice booming down at them. They moved over to the left side of the ship and gripped the railing. In the distance, black smoke rose above the water. Its curling tower of death could mean only one thing; a ship was burning.

"Luc! Take us over there," Captain Montpellier shouted to the helmsman. Walking briskly across the deck, he shouted down into the bowels of the ship, "All hands on deck!"

Curses filled the air alongside the sound of chairs being knocked over and boots pounding on the wooden floors. The crew instantly spotted the smoke upon arriving on deck.

"*Copains*, we're going over to investigate," Captain Montpellier said to the assembled crew. "I have no idea what happened and there may be a ship lurking in the area that caused this, so be prepared for the worst. Gunners to your cannons. Sharpshooters up the ropes to your positions. The rest of you I want on deck in three groups: Bow, midsection, stern. GO!"

The men hustled into their various positions, the ship alive with the fine-tuned choreography of an experienced fighting crew.

Below deck, the gunners peered out the gun ports, anxiously scanning for any sign of a ship. Sharpshooters up top craned their necks in all directions. The men on deck shifted relentlessly, eager to either fight or stand down; waiting was the worst part.

Captain Montpellier compacted his spyglass and put it back in its case. No one had seen any sign of a ship, other than the one that was engulfed in front of them. There was no point in trying to board; the damage was all-consuming. The vessel was clearly about to succumb to the flames and sink. The tattered pirate flag atop it caught fire and rapidly incinerated.

"Captain! Starboard side; Survivors!" one of the sharpshooters called out.

The captain and most of the men on deck rushed to the right side of the ship and looked out at the water. Near the burning ship, clinging to broken pieces of wood, six men were spotted.

"Haul them aboard!" Captain Montpellier called out to the men near the bow.

The six were brought onboard and given blankets, food, and some rum. After speaking to Fontaine, they were given a place to sleep.

Stepping into the captain's quarters, Fontaine closed the door and sat down.

"How are they?" Captain Montpellier inquired.

"They'll be fine. Tired of course. Some burns, cuts and bruises, but nothing too serious."

"What happened?"

"Apparently they had a run-in with the English Navy."

"Ah, the English. The only thing worse than the Spanish Navy, is the English Navy."

"Indeed. Surprised them, caught them totally off guard."

"How did the naval ship surprise them so badly? Wasn't anyone on lookout?"

"Sounds like they had quite a night last night and were sluggish this morning. Just rotten luck that today was the day the naval vessel stumbled upon them. Once the alarm went up, they didn't have enough time to outrun them, so the captain decided to fight it out."

"Didn't go his way?"

"Not at all. The English had the weather gage and superior firepower; conducted themselves quite well. Formidable force, the English."

"*Oui.* Only the six men survived?"

"They said that the English vessel didn't appear interested in prisoners. Pretty withering barrage of fire after the pirates sent over the first volley."

"Is the ship still in the area?"

"No. They said it attacked, destroyed the ship, and then sailed off in the other direction thank god. Didn't stop for survivors, just hit 'em and left. Oh yes, they did say one other thing; the ship's captain appeared quite young."

"Young?"

"Younger than normal."

"Any chance they overheard his name?"

"Hazard, Captain Hazard."

"*Sacre bleu*. Is that really his name?"

Fontaine laughed, "That's what they said."

"Great, that's all we need; an English warship commanded by a brash youngster named 'Hazard' who shows no quarter."

Silence filled the room for a spell until Captain Montpellier smacked the table and said, "Oh well, always going to be something, right cousin. The British are a hard nut to crack, what else is new. We're not going to let this news spoil our fun! Where are we right now?"

Fontaine looked at the large map on the desk, pointed and said, "Roughly here."

Stroking his chin while staring at the map, Captain Montpellier suddenly jabbed his finger against it and said, "There, New Seville. A little over a day's sail with good wind and not too terribly off course from where we're headed. We'll swing in, pay a quick visit to the Crazy Goat, and then drop off the six survivors in town. There's always someone stopping in New Seville looking for more crew members."

"Perfect; I love that tavern! We'll have a few drinks with Genarrio and then be on our way."

PAGE INTENTIONALLY LEFT BLANK

CHAPTER TEN

THE SOUND OF HAMMERING that had filled the wharf at New Seville was still ringing in Captain Montpellier's ears when he started hearing fresh construction work ahead. Arriving at the entrance to the Crazy Goat, he noticed repairs being carried out throughout the establishment. Standing at the bar, a man was looking around with a beaker of rum in his hand.

"Genarrio! My friend, how are you?" Montpellier called out, briskly approaching the man and enveloping him in a giant hug.

"I am well Captain Montpellier, thank you. Tired, but well."

"So I see. Sprucing up the place, eh? Very nice!"

"We're not 'sprucing it up;' two crews were in here a couple of nights ago and tore the place to shit!"

"Oh, I am sorry my friend. Which crews?"

"Umberland and that strange Dutch guy... Van Muis."

"I like Umberland; he's a good man. Good captain."

"Yeah, I like Umberland too. Not right now, but I like him."

"What happened? What set it off?"

"Apparently one of our regulars was bouncing between Umberland and Van Muis and set the whole thing off."

"Who?"

"Savannah."

Captain Montpellier let out an enormous laugh and said, "Hurricane!? That crazy woman. No wonder things got... what?"

Genarrio had begun quickly motioning with one hand for him to be quiet.

"And which 'crazy woman' might you be referring to darlin'?" a voice called out, accompanied by the sound of approaching footsteps.

Genarrio closed his eyes for a second as Captain Montpellier turned around and said with an exaggerated flourish of one arm, "Miss Savannah Hurricane, a thousand apologies. Please remember that I'm just a rude Frenchman."

"Now you're being redundant honey."

Genarrio chuckled as Savannah insisted on a drink being bought for her. A whiskey was promptly in her hand.

Taking her hand in his, Captain Montpellier said, "Please excuse us my dear, but I must speak with the gentleman alone for a minute."

Pulling her hand away, Savannah replied, "Suit yourself, you guys are boring me anyway."

Turning, she walked over to the table of two scallywags, sat down on the lap of one of them and began speaking to the other, both already firmly in the palm of her hand.

"So what's up?" Genarrio asked as the two stepped outside.

"We fished six men out of the water next to a burning ship recently, the only survivors of a pirate crew that got cut to pieces by a Royal Navy vessel. The ship's captain is a younger fellow named Hazard."

"Never heard of him."

"Nor I. Spread the word to those you see; apparently young Mr. Hazard showed no quarter. Sounds like he's a bit of a loose cannon; brash but formidable."

"Will do. Thanks for the heads up."

"You be careful out there yourself my friend."

"I'll be as careful as you are."

Both men laughed and headed back inside.

In the middle of the room, two of the female regulars sat at a small round table consuming tankards of beer. Jenny was 21 with medium-length brown hair that fell over one shoulder. Alice was three years younger and had blonde hair that cascaded down her back like a waterfall. Both had moved to the Caribbean with their respective families when they were younger, only to rebel and set out on their own. Jenny watched over Alice like a protective older sister, though both were experienced with the island's rougher element.

After taking a long drink, Jenny set the tankard down and said, "I don't know Alice. I just can't shake it."

"What's that Jen?"

"The feeling that there has to be more to life than this. There just *has* to be!"

"I hear ya."

"I mean is this it? Are we just here to drink and have men harass us?"

"You don't like the fellas?"

"I like them enough, and some are really sweet, but I just mean in general. Sit here, meet a fella, get married, have kids, grow old and die. Is that it? Surely there's more than that."

"Hey, quiet down sugar tits," a man two tables over called out to them. Letting out a laugh, he continued, "Why don't you come over here and sit on my lap? Life will seem better."

"Fuck you!" Alice snapped, but her words were lost on him as he reacted with surprise at Jenny leaping to her feet, swiftly crossing the distance between them and laying him out with four proper punches to the face.

She kicked the unconscious man in the stomach, as Genarrio shouted to two of the repairmen, "Get that sack of shit outta here!"

Running over, they picked up the man, dragged him to the door and tossed him into the street.

"Sorry ladies," he said to Jenny and Alice. "No one talks like that to two of my favorite customers. Lupe! Two fresh tankards for the ladies, on the house."

"Coming right up. Love you Jen!"

"Love you too Lupe."

Setting the fresh beers in front of them, Lupe grabbed both of Jenny's hands and admired the bloody red knuckles on each one. "God, I love that you can hit with both hands. That was awesome."

"Thanks luv. I've seen you toss out the trash yourself."

Lupe laughed, winked, and headed back behind the bar.

"Cheers!" Alice hollered. They slammed tankards and took long pulls.

"So you're not happy?" she continued.

"It's not that I'm not happy," Jenny responded. "It's just that I want *more*. More! I want adventure! I want to experience more than just cooking, cleaning, and catering to the every wish of some man."

"Hun you don't know how to cook."

"Shut up you brat! You know what I mean."

Alice laughed. "Yeah, I know what you mean."

"Listen Alice, I am going to have adventure in my life! And so are you! There's so much more to this world than our current situation. We are going to have so many rich, amazing experiences! But we have to make the life that we want for ourselves. If we just sit here, nothing will ever happen. We'll walk through that door tomorrow and 30 years will have passed. If we want more from this life, we have to take it!"

"I wonder where we'll be in five years."

"We'll be in far better circumstances. We'll be flying high."

"Yeah!"

The two slammed tankards again and downed the rest of their beers in a mighty pull, heads thrown fully back.

Alice missed the table when she tried to set her tankard down and it fell into her lap. Both burst out laughing and Jenny shouted to the bar, "Lupe my luv! Two more!"

"You two haven't changed one bit. I love that about you," a voice said while setting two tankards on the table a few minutes later.

"Montpellier!" Alice cried out, jumping up and throwing her arms around him.

"And how are two of the most beautiful women in all the Caribbean doing on this fine day?"

"Oh stop. Bet you say that to all the women."

"Alice my love, I call many different women many different things, but 'most beautiful' is a term I reserve for an exceptionally small group that you and Jenny are very much among."

Both women smiled at Montpellier and Jenny rose to hug him as well.

"What brings you to New Seville?" Alice asked.

"A monumental raid! Crazy end to it, but still one of the finest of our career," Montpellier responded, gesturing to Fontaine at the bar.

"And you came here to celebrate? I would have thought you'd head to Borracho," Jenny said.

"That's exactly where we're headed actually. Got detoured here after stumbling upon a destroyed pirate ship with a few survivors. And what a stroke of luck it turned out to be; we get to visit with you two lovelies."

"How many survivors?"

"Six"

"That's it?"

"Brash young English captain named Hazard tore them to pieces apparently."

"Hmm... shame."

"That's the life luv. Sometimes the wind blows against you."

"Indeed."

"To the lost!" Alice interjected, raising her tankard high, spilling a bit on the table.

"To the lost!" Montpellier and Jenny exclaimed, also raising their tankards above their heads. All three took long pulls.

"So, you're heading to Borracho eh?" Jenny said, arching her eyebrow as she looked at Montpellier.

"Yes…"

"Soon it sounds like."

"Yeah. Why?"

"Don't suppose there's room onboard for the two of us to hitch along with you?"

"Jenny!" Alice exclaimed.

"Oh hush! We were just talking about wanting more adventure in our lives; what's more adventurous than this!?"

"Borracho is no place for girls like you, you should listen to Alice."

"First off, we're not girls; we're women. Second, we can take care of ourselves there! Alice; you're in, right?"

"Oh… of course!" Alice responded hesitantly.

"Excellent! It's settled!"

"Not quite. My apologies, but the answer is still no."

"Why?" Jenny said, taking a drink from her tankard.

"I think the world of you two and admire your courage and love of adventure. Reminds me of… me. But as fine as my crew is, I cannot guarantee your safety onboard, even for a few days. The fellas would get distracted, jealous. There is just too much potential for it to end badly."

"It's not fair! We're not doing anything wrong," Alice said, the smile disappearing from her face.

"Of course not my dear; you're doing nothing wrong. It's the lads, not you. Same the world over."

"Men."

"I'm sorry to have to decline, but I must insist. We cannot take you."

"Very well then Captain," Jenny said. She finished her tankard in a mighty pull, handed him the empty vessel, and dismissively continued, "Be a dear and fetch us two more of these. Then we must insist on some privacy; we have a trip to plan."

"Wait Jenny, I'm not finished with mine yet."

"Well then you had better drink up, and drink fast! Two more Montpellier! We'll see you in Borracho!"

Montpellier smiled as wide as he could and headed to the bar.

Returning with the two tankards, he picked up the empty one that Alice had just managed to finish in time. Kissing her hand, he said, "You are two of the most amazing women I've ever met. Ladies, it's been an absolute pleasure, and I count the minutes until we meet again… wherever that may be."

He kissed Jenny on each cheek, bowed regally, and returned to the bar to drink with Fontaine.

The next day found him at the Crazy Goat again, drinking with Genarrio and Fontaine.

"Genarrio! One last drink before we head out my old friend."

"Who are you calling old?!"

"Shut up and drink!"

The three of them burst out laughing and downed their beakers of rum.

"Be well good sirs," Genarrio said, hugging each man.

"Thank you as always, for your generous hospitality," Fontaine responded.

"Until we meet again, may fortune smile upon you!" Captain Montpellier exclaimed grandly.

"And to you as well!"

Fontaine and Montpellier headed back to the dock, bid farewell to the six men they had saved, and boarded the *Cheval*.

The six injured men waved at the ship as it eased away from the pier and headed out to sea.

"Luc! Head us to Borracho, where we'll feast like kings!"

The crew shouted in agreement and hustled to their various stations as the wind caught the sails.

The vessel surged forward, as if the weather gods themselves approved of the destination.

CHAPTER ELEVEN

THE *Cheval* was making good time. It was three hours past noon, and the wind was blowing strong in their favor. Up in the Crow's Nest, Sampson swept the area in front of them with his spyglass. All was clear. Smiling, he stretched his arms out wide. A snake tattoo wrapped its way up his left arm from the wrist to the shoulder. The head faced the hand and knuckles, its mouth fully open. The two fangs seemed almost real. The tattoo hid a nasty scar seared into his arm; a souvenir from the beast he was unlucky enough to have had as a father. His mother had been taken by the plague when he was just eight, depriving his house of all love and compassion. For six harsh years, he'd endured his father's depraved beatings. As soon as he turned 14, he fled the house of horrors and took to the sea, joining a pirate crew the moment he arrived in the Caribbean. Now 18 years of age, being part of the crew provided a sense of family. He had brothers who loved him and whom he loved as well. Though the life could be harsh and unforgiving at times, he wouldn't trade it for anything.

Lowering his arms, Sampson looked ahead of the ship. They were still a full day's sail from Borracho, but he could already hear the celebrations and taste the delicious concoctions. He couldn't wait to arrive; there was no place like Borracho.

The sounds of Coqauvin and Rhodes practicing swordplay on the deck below returned his thoughts to the present. Looking over the edge, he watched as far below, the two worked on their technique. Coqauvin was taller and stronger, but Rhodes was definitely faster. Despite being only 5'4" and of slim build, Rhodes could deliver a strike with pinpoint accuracy. Coqauvin jumped back twice and exclaimed in pain both times the tip of Rhodes' blade pricked his arm. Finally, roaring as he went, he charged the smaller man and forced him against the side of the ship. Lifting him off the ground, he threatened to toss him overboard as Rhodes punched him repeatedly against the ribs.

Some of the others around laughed at them, and Sampson shouted down that Coqauvin should do it. Pushing each other as they separated, Rhodes and Coqauvin moved back into position to start again. Breaking his gaze from the two, Sampson stretched his arms out wide again and smiled as he looked around, his huge mane of hair flowing over his shoulders. But the smile dropped as quickly as it had appeared as his gaze fell on the tall sails of the ship behind them. Raising his spyglass, he froze at the image he saw. The ship was still a ways behind them, but it was moving fast. And though he could barely make it out, the flag was unmistakable.

Down on the deck, Rhodes and Coqauvin halted at the sound of the voice yelling at them from the Crow's Nest. Heading to the side of the ship, Coqauvin stared at the distant sails behind them and then broke into a sprint across the deck. Flying down the stairs, he was immediately directed to the captain.

"What news Coqauvin?" Captain Montpellier said, immediately knowing it was bad.

"A ship flying the flag of Great Britain has been spotted behind us Captain. She's closing fast!"

Rushing to the deck, Captain Montpellier raised his spyglass and cursed at the approaching English warship.

"Is it Hazard?" Fontaine called out as he emerged onto the deck.

"How am I supposed to know!? His name isn't written on the flag, only our deaths are."

Thundering up the stairs to the Quarterdeck, Captain Montpellier ordered the sails out full and told Luc to hold their present course.

For over an hour, the two ships sailed as fast as they could. Despite the many talents of the pirate crew, their ship simply wasn't up to the task of outrunning the naval vessel that was pursuing them. As the hour passed four in the afternoon, the distance between them was noticeably shortening.

Standing on the Quarterdeck, Captain Montpellier surveyed the crew working as hard as possible to nurse any additional speed from the sails. The wind had increased and the water was turning choppy. Closing his eyes, Montpellier partially extended his arms and spread his fingers out on either hand. He felt the wind blowing over his forearms and hitting the tips of the fingers. With his eyes shut tight, he focused on every nuance he was feeling from them.

Opening his eyes, he looked out at the sky. As was typical in this part of the world, the late afternoon was bringing a storm. Clouds had taken over the sky and the wind was increasing. Montpellier smiled.

Five minutes later, the rain began to fall. It wasn't a gentle rain like in songs and tales; it was a pounding rain that seemed to start in an instant.

Montpellier barked fresh orders to the crew and stood right next to Luc at the wheel. Fontaine was below him, running orders back and forth across the deck. The ship curved from side to side, guided by Montpellier's natural talent for sailing during rough weather. He seemed to sense the waves and continually provided Luc with instructions on which way to turn the wheel, as well as what he wanted the crew to do.

The afternoon spring storms in the Caribbean typically lasted less than half an hour, and usually no more than 15 minutes. However during that time, the wind and rain struck with a fury.

Looking behind him, Captain Montpellier could see the distance growing between him and his pursuer. He never left Luc's side during the 22-minute storm. The crew performed valiantly in the driving rain and were rewarded for their efforts with a valuable lead. As quickly as it had started, the rain stopped. Within a few minutes, the clouds had parted and the sun shone brightly as it headed towards its daily demise.

Captain Montpellier ordered anything non-essential to be thrown overboard. Time was on their side, but they could count on no more favors. Now it was a race; if they could stay far enough ahead of the warship until dark, they could lose her once night fell.

After more than two agonizing hours of pushing the ship to go as fast as possible, the sun mercifully dipped below the horizon. Never had the crew been more thankful to see the stars. Montpellier order all lights kept off and immediately changed course. After a while, they changed course again.

As midnight approached, Montpellier and Fontaine were drinking wine on the darkened deck.

"Do you think it was Hazard?" Fontaine asked. "Perhaps he spotted us picking up the survivors."

"Perhaps. Perhaps it was just bad luck."

"Maybe he was waiting outside New Seville for us to leave."

"It's possible, but I don't think so. I have no clue who it was, but he definitely was determined. I was hoping he would break off the chase after the rain stopped, but the man kept at it until the sun went down."

"Thankfully it's spring. In a few more months, the sun would have been up for another two hours."

Montpellier nodded and took a sip from the goblet in his hand.

"Listen Fontaine," he said after a few minutes had passed. "There is something we have to do. I don't want to do it, but we have to."

Fontaine nodded as the captain spoke and then let out a laugh, "You're kidding, right?"

"Nope."

"Oh come on! That's something people talk about us doing, but I don't know anyone who actually *does* it."

"Well we're going to."

Several hours later, the morning sun brought the ship to life once again as Luc steered her in the direction Montpellier had instructed.

"I thought we were heading to Borracho?" he said while sipping his morning wine.

"We are, but we have to make a stop first."

"Tell him why!" Fontaine shouted from the deck below.

"Shut up! Just steer the boat Luc. I'll explain when we get there."

Two hours later, the lookout shouted that land was in sight.

Luc expertly navigated the ship into the shallows and the anchor was tossed into the water. With the ship secured, Montpellier ordered the crew on deck.

"What are we doing here Captain?" Sampson called out, looking over at the island.

"*Copains*, soon we will be in Borracho, where we will celebrate raiding the Spanish, as well as our hard-earned escape from the English!"

Cheers greeted his words by the crew.

"However, before we go to Borracho, we must stop here and bury some of the treasure we plundered."

Murmurs broke out from a few of the crew and quizzical looks were thrown the captain's way.

"*Copains*, we all love Borracho. There is nowhere in the entire world like that wild island. However, part of what makes it amazing is also why we must bury some of this loot. It's simply too much money to have sitting in the hold of the ship on an island with so many scallywags. And as yesterday proved, danger lurks in many places for us. We must have a reserve, just in case."

The crew mostly nodded in agreement and prepared the two small boats to row the treasure over to the island. One asked the captain where they were, but he merely smiled and patted the man on the shoulder.

Two chests of gold and silver were left onboard the *Cheval* to be divided equally amongst the crew. The other two were placed on one of the two small boats and taken to the island by Captain Montpellier, Fontaine and six others. Luc was put in charge of the ship, as was usual when the captain and first mate weren't on it.

"Are you going to mark the spot with a stupid X?" Fontaine mockingly asked Montpellier as they watched three of the men digging away.

"Complain all you want; this has to be done."

"And just how will you remember where in all this jungle we buried it?"

Montpellier smiled wide at Fontaine and winked.

"Oh, that helps."

Montpellier broke out laughing as the crew paused and looked at him.

"Keep digging *copains*. An extra ration of rum for you upon our return!"

Smiling, the three went back to work.

Upon completion, the two chests were placed at the bottom of the hole. They were fully covered with dirt, and then more dirt thrown on top of that layer until the hole was half-full. Then, the dirt was patted down hard to form a new "floor" onto which Captain Montpellier placed three cloth bags of silver coins surrounded by small rocks. The remainder of the hole was filled with dirt, patted down again, and then disguised with various scrubs and grass. Montpellier told the crew to relax in the shade before they headed back to the *Cheval*, while he and Fontaine took a quick hike.

The two of them climbed partially up the mountain that formed the heart of the uninhabited island. Montpellier stopped when they reached a pair of rocks that sat on a natural ledge of the mountainside and gestured for Fontaine to join him. Hopping on top of the rocks, they looked out at the impossibly beautiful blue water of the Caribbean that stretched out before them.

Gently sitting in the water near the island was the *Cheval*, looking like a toy in a giant bathtub. Flying proudly above the ship was the flag Montpellier and Fontaine had designed themselves with the approval of the crew.

The flag was black with the familiar skull and crossed swords design in the middle of it. Below the swords were four bottles; three were upright, the last was tipped over. The skull and swords represented the crew's willingness to fight when needed. The four bottles stood for the crew fully embracing life and a love of adventure. For Montpellier and Fontaine, they also indicated that they were 4th generation scallywags. The tipped over bottle represented the inevitable fate we all face when the final curtain falls.

"I never get tired of how stunning the water is in this part of the world," Fontaine said.

"One of the most majestic sights on this amazing planet for sure. But do you see anything else?"

"I see our ship."

"Anything else?"

"What?! I see the mountain and the jungle and the water. What is it?"

Montpellier broke into a huge smile and stood right next to Fontaine. Extending his arm, he pointed down to the jungle below them.

"You have to know what you're looking for cousin. To see it, you must be standing in this exact spot at this exact time of the day. Look at how the sunlight illuminates those rocks in the water that lead to the island. Then follow that line through the jungle until you hit the start of the mountain. See how the sunlight illuminates the tops of the trees that stand a bit above the rest? Now look to the other side where those two palm trees are growing at a steep angle over the water's edge. Follow that line until you reach the cluster of coconut trees near the mountain. As you're following that line, concentrate hard and you'll spot where it meets the illuminated treetops from the first line I showed you. Now what do you see?"

Fontaine looked back and forth a few times in frustration from the points that had been described. Suddenly he gasped slightly and looked quickly over at Montpellier's grinning face.

"Oh my God, they form an X. And we buried the treasure…"

"Exactly where the two meet cousin. So what was it you were saying earlier about a stupid X?"

Fontaine broke into a laugh and looked away.

"Who is the best cousin? *Who* is the best?"

"You are Montpellier," Fontaine said, slapping him on the shoulder. "Always."

"All right then! Let's grab the others and head back to the boat! Now we can finally sail to Borracho and feast until we collapse!"

Part 4:

Borracho

PAGE INTENTIONALLY LEFT BLANK

CHAPTER TWELVE

"BORRACHO!" the man in the *Cheval's* crow's nest shouted down to the deck the following day, pointing triumphantly towards the landmass just barely visible in front of them.

The island was large enough to contain the main town of Ciudad Borracho in the north, as well as three smaller villages: South, East, and West. The pirates who originally settled the island figured simplicity was the best strategy when it came to naming the villages, and they were right. The four settlements comprised the points of the compass and could serve as reinforced strongholds if needed.

Hills surrounded the island. In the middle stood a decent-sized lake; one could row across it in under an hour. Channels had been created that allowed ships to sail from the sea to the lake in two directions. This enabled the pirates to have an escape route if attacked, as well as the ability to lure invaders to their doom by leading them to the middle of the island where cannons were positioned on all sides.

The tallest peak could be climbed in a little over an hour and contained the island's primary lookout post. A system of lighted torches could be used to signal trouble from each of the towns, though it was generally understood that naval warships preferred to hunt the pirates individually rather than attempt an assault on such a heavily defended target.

Virtually every established pirate knew of Borracho and visited often. If a pirate captain was trying to get a message to another captain, leaving word at a pub in Ciudad Borracho was often the best way. Unless someone specified that they were in one of the smaller villages, it was assumed that they meant Ciudad Borracho when they said they were going to Borracho.

After tossing their ropes to the men on the pier, the *Cheval* was secured and Captain Montpellier stepped ashore.

"No Southern French pretty boys are allowed here! Be gone with you!" a voice shouted out behind him.

Turning slowly, he put his hand on the hilt of his sword, narrowed his eyes at the man standing in the middle of the pier and said, "Fuck you, you uncultured Polish dog!"

Both men stood facing each other as the dock workers stared at them nervously.

Simultaneously, they broke into huge grins and relaxed their stances. "Captain Jacques Montpellier! You've returned!" the man in the middle of the pier exclaimed, throwing his arms out wide.

"Captain Jaconavich Piwoski! So good to see you again my friend!"

The two embraced and each banged their fist on the back of the other.

"I haven't seen you in months! How have you been?" Piwoski said.

"I have been spectacular! Man do I have a story to tell you about the adventures we just had!"

"Excellent! Once you get settled, I'm staying at Ye Olde Rustic Inn. Meet me there tonight around 6 and we'll rage!"

"That place sucks!" Fontaine shouted as he stepped onto the pier, a bottle of wine in his hand.

"Fuck you wine-slurper!" Piwoski shot back.

Fontaine broke out laughing as the two embraced. He took a pull from the bottle and passed it around.

"Montpellier tells me that you all had quite an adventure recently."

"A couple of them actually; the raid and then almost dying."

"Almost dying?"

"That's right!" Montpellier interjected. "I totally forgot to tell you."

"Tell me what?"

"As we were heading here after conducting the raid that I'll tell you about tonight, we ran across a burning pirate ship."

"Which one?"

"The six survivors we plucked out of the water said it was called *Good Fortune*. Captain's name was Bridgeport."

"Vaguely recall the name. Was he one of the survivors?"

"Nupe, didn't make it. But the thing I wanted to tell you was who destroyed his ship. Apparently, there's a new young captain with the English Royal Navy named 'Hazard.' Showed no quarter after the pirates sent across the first volley. Then we ran into an English warship that may have been commanded by this young lad, and she almost had the better of us."

"Not quite the news I was hoping to hear."

"Nor I. Spread the word around would you? We'll do the same."

"Just another thing to watch out for, but definitely good to spread the word."

"Yeah, always something right?"

"Always."

Bidding farewell until later, the two parted company with Captain Piwoski, paid the "donation" fee for docking, and headed off to visit the captain.

Reaching the upper reaches of Ciudad Borracho, they approached a sprawling estate. A low stone wall surrounded the property solely for decorative purposes; it was waist-high at best. Two cobblestone paths curved across the expansive lawn leading up to the two-story Spanish-style villa.

The roof was lined with red tiles that contrasted beautifully with the cream-colored exterior walls and marble pillars. Magnificent archways lined both the lower and upper pathways that encircled the structure. In the front facing the town, two short round towers stood on either end reaching just above the roof.

Crossing the lawn, they ascended the five stone steps and knocked on the wooden door. After waiting a minute, Fontaine grabbed the handle of the brass bell that stood on the right side of the doorframe and gave it three hard clangs.

A man appeared and let them in. Instructing them to wait in the foyer, he headed off.

"Decent pad," Fontaine quipped, surveying the high walls and ornate ceiling.

"It better be; he captured the entire treasury at Porto Bello and spent a month looting the town. He then received a massive ransom to leave. That alone netted him more gold than one could spend in two lifetimes, not to mention all the other treasure he acquired throughout his career."

"Best of the best, no doubt about that."

Montpellier nodded and headed over to inspect one of the many statues. He nodded admirably at the figure of Poseidon, standing triumphantly on top of a wave holding his trident high. A booming voice yanked him away from the statue and over to the figure standing in the far doorway. "Captain Jacques Montpellier! You have returned!"

"Captain Henry Morgan! Wonderful to be back!"

The two embraced and then Captain Morgan approached Fontaine and welcomed him back as well.

Leading them out back, he paused and said, "Lagoon or beer hall?"

"My good Captain, it is your estate; we insist you choose," Montpellier replied.

"Beer hall!"

The cobblestone path curved along the far edge of the lagoon, which occupied more than half of the rear section of the estate. The water was a rich blue, expanding across an area large enough for both of Morgan's 20-person boats to sail comfortably around it. An island stood in the middle with two small hills containing interconnecting caves. The tales of what took place on that little patch of earth during what Morgan referred to as "Our Nights With Dionysius," are too scandalous to tell here.

Passing the lagoon, the path veered left to the beer hall. The round sandstone building occupied two levels. On the outside, a wide twisting staircase led from the ground to the second level. Columns lined the upper balcony that wrapped around the structure. In the section that faced west, a rectangular piece jutted out. Wide enough for three round 2-seater tables, it marked the perfect spot for having an afternoon drink while the sun set. Similar small tables were set out around the upper balcony. Tall, arched windows surrounded the building on both levels.

The inside of the second level was a replica of a German beer hall. The ceiling was high with dark wooden beams along the top of it, as well as across the front and back walls. Spread out across the room were five long, wooden tables with benches on either side that could seat 20 people each. On one end of the room stood a stage for the musicians. On the other end, running virtually the entire width, was a bar with eight massive taps. During the many festivities held there, barrels upon barrels of beer filled the area, with stout women running the massive tankards to those in attendance. Running dry was never a fear, for directly next to the estate was a brewer in Morgan's employment. On the lower level, large grills cooked tons of sausage, chicken and pork. Dumbwaiters connected the two levels, expediting the serving process. A nearby baker was available to constantly run over hearty pretzels and rolls as well.

On this day however, it was just the three of them. Heading upstairs, Captain Morgan guided them to the rectangular area facing west. Steins of beer along with plates of sausage, chicken, onions, pickles, bread and spicy mustard were promptly delivered to them.

"*Prost!*" they shouted, banging their steins together and drinking deeply.

"Montpellier! Regale me with tales of your latest adventure. I always love hearing about your exploits."

"Well, you know Fontaine and I come from a family of rogues of course."

"Indeed. Fourth generation scallywags if memory serves me correctly."

"Exactly! Our grandfather Andre plundered the Southern French coast for many years and passed all he knew on to our father, who passed it on to us. Our great-grandfather was the original family rogue."

"Your Great Aunt Sophie was quite a lady as well from what I've heard."

Both burst out laughing and Fontaine said, "I'll say! She successfully bedded, then robbed, over a dozen nobles. Got more treasure than Grandpa or Great-Grandpa ever did!"

All three laughed as Montpellier continued, "While Great Aunt Sophie was scandalous indeed, the one heist that we heard about the most was the story of our uncle Yves."

A smile filled Fontaine's face as he nodded in agreement.

"Now Uncle Yves wasn't quite as successful as our father or grandfather. Actually, for quite a while he was a bit of an embarrassment."

"The local authorities called him *Ane*," Fontaine added.

"*Ane*?" Morgan inquired, taking a pull from his beer.

"Means 'jackass.'"

Morgan smiled and shook his head, "One in every family."

"Yeah, that was definitely Yves."

Montpellier then proceeded to relay the story of their Uncle Yves' famous heist, as well as their recent adventure plundering part of the treasury at Santa Fermin.

When he was finished, Fontaine described their encounter with the English warship and what they knew about Captain Hazard.

"To your scandalous family!" Morgan exclaimed when the stories had ended.

They all banged their tankards together, finished them in one go and hollered for the next round.

After more stories were told, and more beer consumed, they graciously thanked him for his hospitality. Montpellier presented Captain Morgan with some choice items from the treasure they had plundered, and then they took their leave.

PAGE INTENTIONALLY LEFT BLANK

CHAPTER THIRTEEN

ON BORRACHO, the significance of the sun setting was similar to the significance of it rising in most other parts of the world. People woke from slumbered, hungover sleep and prepared for the next night's revelry. Restaurants opened for business, pubs roared to life and whorehouses prepared for the coming visitors. All across the island, the night dominated the day.

"Montpellier, let's start here!" Captain Piwoski called out, gesturing towards a brightly-lit two-story building. The sign next to the door read: The Sunken Vessel.

Bursting through door, Piwoski commandeered two tables, ordered his three companions to sit and then roared at the startled bartender, "Four tankards of your finest beer for the best damn pirates on this godforsaken island!"

Montpellier, Fontaine and Piwoski's first mate Zygmunt burst out laughing and shouted, "Huzzah!"

"Here's to living life to the fullest!" Piwoski declared, holding his tankard high.

The other three echoed the statement, clinked tankards, banged them on the table and took long pulls.

The pub was narrow, but deep. The four of them were on the right side, sitting at tables along the back wall facing the bar. Two small tables were by the front windows with the entrance between them. The kitchen was in the back and there was a staircase before the kitchen that led up to the main level.

"See that fish?" a man at the table next to them called out, spilling his beer slightly while pointing to a large swordfish above the bar.

"Yeah," said Fontaine, typically annoyed by drunken strangers interrupting them.

"The owner once killed a man with that thing."

"Bullshit."

"It's true! I was here that night. I saw it all!"

"You look like you wouldn't be able to see Captain Morgan himself if he walked in here right now," Piwoski chimed in.

"Who?"

Fontaine shook his head and turned his attention back to his beer.

"Hey Lucas, did you ever kill a man with that fish?" the drunk man said to the man behind the bar.

"Yes I did, Your Majesty."

"Your Majesty?" Zygmunt inquired.

"That's right lads, you currently have the honor of speaking with our island's beloved royalty, Emperor Sandbar I."

Piwoski finished a long drink and said, "So how are you the Emperor?"

Emperor Sandbar I stood up majestically, walked to the bar, laid a piece of paper on it and saluted the owner, who returned the salute.

"It's time for me to take my leave good subjects. Until next time, enjoy my benevolent kingdom," he said with a grand wave of his arm and stumbled out the door.

"What the hell just happened?!" Piwoski asked, staring at the owner confused.

Out the window, they could see a few people saluting him on the street.

"Poor fellow," Lucas said, taking the piece of paper off the bar. "Here, keep this as a souvenir."

Montpellier walked over to him and grabbed the paper. Holding it up, he read it aloud: *"Imperial Note of His Majesty, Emperor Sandbar I, Ruler of the Caribbean. This note serves as payment for goods or services rendered, by order of the Emperor."*

"So what's the story?" Piwoski asked Lucas, taking the note from Montpellier.

"He was a pirate originally, of course. Came in here about 10 years ago flush from an extremely successful raiding expedition and started throwing his money around lavishly. Somewhere on the island he heard the rumor about the lost gold of Old Havana and became obsessed with finding it. He spent days talking to every old drunk he could find and was convinced that he had found out where it was."

Here Lucas paused and shook his head sadly. He poured himself a whiskey and took a small sip.

Everyone downstairs was silent, waiting for him to continue.

"He took off with a crew of over 200 men spread across three ships. The month was… April. Nine months later a supply ship arrived, and he limped off it, aged far beyond his years. He dragged himself to the nearest hotel and collapsed. For two days and two nights he laid there in his bed. No food, no water, nothing. He was near death when the proprietor broken down the door and found him. Thank God he had only paid for two nights or he would have died in that room. Seeing the condition he was in, the proprietor had him carried to a doctor, after lifting the last of his money from his pockets. Seeing the young man prematurely aged, the doctor took pity on him and along with his wife, nursed him back to health. When he walked out of the doctor's house after recovering, he declared himself Emperor Sandbar I, Ruler of the Caribbean, and began handing out these pieces of paper as 'Imperial Notes.' Most of us have grown fond of him and give him some beer or food. He is always around and serves as a good source of information about all that goes on here."

"What happened to his expedition?" one of the people by the window asked.

"After searching for a few months, a hurricane hit them weeks before the first ones usually appear. Wiped out all three ships; stranded him and the few survivors on some island. Apparently things got pretty bad there. Affected him a lot. He's never talked about it, I only know because he told the doctor once during his recovery."

Finishing his beer, Fontaine said, "Let's get out of here."

Piwoski agreed and they finished their beers in one go.

Taking the "Imperial Note" with them, they headed out into the night.

Fireworks were being fired from the beach and exploding over a floating barge near the shore full of dancing men and women. Gypsy musicians were filling the air with their amazing guitar playing. Gypsy guitar is truly one of the most unique sounds in the musical world and when played fast, is simply the best possible sound for festivities. It fills the atmosphere with a fun vibe and is perfect for dancing.

The four of them looked at the group dancing on the barge and burst out laughing as one fell over the side. Those near him on the barge joined the laughter while pretending to help him back onboard. Finally relenting, they let him grab someone's arm and pulled him up.

The group ventured deeper into town and were approaching their next destination when Fontaine suddenly yelled, "LOOK OUT!"

Eight people had burst out of a pub to their left and were chasing each other into the street. The bodies were a whirl of punches, kicks, groans and curses. Two of the participants started to dominate the fight, knocking two of their opponents unconscious, stabbing a third and chasing away two more. The final opponent was chased down, swung between them, and then tossed through a window.

Shouting cries of victory, they hurled threats at the onlookers and hugged each other in the middle of the street.

"Jenny?! Alice!?" Montpellier shouted, breaking from the group and running up to them.

"Montpellier!" Alice shouted upon spotting him. Rushing forward, she interrupted his question by giving him a huge hug.

Jenny stood back, looking at him aloofly with her arms crossed.

"Who are these stunning ladies?" Piwoski asked, stepping forward.

Montpellier introduced them, and Piwoski complemented them on their fighting prowess.

"We're heading just up the road to the Old Pub; I insist you join us!" he said.

"The Old Pub is for old men," Jenny replied. "*You* follow *us* back inside the Hurricane's Fury!"

"They won't let you back in there!" Zygmunt said.

"Who is this fool!?" Jenny inquired, looking at Montpellier.

"That fellow is Captain Piwoski's first mate; his name is Zygmunt. Be nice to him."

Arching an eyebrow, Jenny looked him up and down and then said, "You need a new name. I'm going to call you... Babushka."

"Jenny! I said be nice to him."

"I *am*. He hasn't been thrown through the window has he? Babushka! You have much to learn. Follow us and be prepared to drink better than you speak."

Leading the group back into the pub they had recently exited, the proprietor took one look at her and Alice and said, "Stop right there! I want to be the first to congratulate you for kicking those six guys' asses!"

Throwing an arm around each woman, he burst out laughing when he heard about the two who had run away at the end of the fight. Jenny placed her hand on the proprietor's muscular black arm and said to her new companions, "Fellas, this is Cannon. Cannon, this is Captain Montpellier, his first mate Fontaine, Captain...what was your name again honey?"

"Captain Jaconavich Piwoski."

"Right; him and his first mate Babushka."

"Babushka?"

"My name's Zygmunt."

"I call him Babushka," Jenny said. "Fellas, Cannon owns one of the absolute best pubs in all of Borracho!"

"That's what we heard about the last place," Zygmunt said.

"Quiet Babushka! What did I tell you about drinking not speaking?"

Zygmunt just shook his at her like she was crazy, and Fontaine let out a laugh.

"Why are you called Cannon?" Montpellier asked.

Turning away from the group, he walked over to a solid wooden table and smashed right through it with one punch. Turning back to them, he saw the familiar sight of eyes wide open.

"Damn," was all Fontaine could get out.

Nodding impressively, Montpellier complimented him and expressed their gratitude for being in his pub.

Smiling in response, he led them to two tables nearby, telling a pair of drunks at one of them to get lost.

The Hurricane's Fury was a large room with four-seater tables throughout it. Roughly 100 people could fit in it, although more often crammed in on particularly raucous nights. Giant chandeliers holding a dozen hearty candles hung from multiple locations on the ceiling. In the middle of the room stood a raised pavilion that could accommodate an additional 20 people. The sign above it read: The Angel's Nest. Ladies danced from the platforms that jutted out on all sides of it, as well as worked the room. Two 10-step staircases led up to the pavilion; smaller tables were set up on it, as well as shelves on either side for setting drinks on. Near the pavilion was a staircase that led down to the 30-person basement section called "The Demon Hole." A second bar served that area, which was kept deliberately darker and smokier. It consisted of a square room with two small alcoves. Cannon described the pub as representing Earth during a hurricane. In the main room, tons of pirates and whores gathered together, drinking, yelling, laughing, dancing and fighting—like the fury and noise of the storms. The pavilion represented a sort of peaceful calm, while the lower bar represented a version of Hell. And just like in a real hurricane, the night wind blew erratically; one never knew which section of the establishment they would end up in. Besides the main room and upper / lower sections, one could also walk out the back door, cross a small alley, and arrive at a two-story structure that served as the pub's brothel.

Two bar wenches promptly brought over a round of beers to their group, and Piwoski gave a celebratory toast to Jenny and Alice's victory.

"Speaking of that," Montpellier said, setting his beer down. "How the hell did you get here?"

"Oh sweetie, do you think you have the only ship in the Caribbean?" Alice asked.

"Of course not. Who brought you here?"

"Merchant ship bringing supplies here. We hitched a ride later on the same day that you refused to take us!"

"That was a stupid move! You two could have gotten hurt pulling a stunt like that!"

Alice let out a laugh and said, "Show him our new good luck charm."

Jenny pulled out a small cloth coin sack and dropped it on the table, staring straight at Montpellier.

"Dare I inquire?" he responded, seeing her steely gaze.

"Crew member's balls... what's left of them."

Montpellier's eyes grew wide as he stared at the sack. The other four men at the tabled wore similar expressions.

Looking back at Jenny, Montpellier composed himself and said, "Got a little too friendly did he?"

"A few of them did. That ended quickly."

Nodding in agreement, Montpellier's look of concern transformed into a wide smile. Raising his tankard, he said, "Zero fucks given. Bastards got what they deserved. Here's to both of you! Two of the most amazing women I've ever met!"

The ladies smiled wide and raised their tankards, and the group took long pulls from their beers.

Round One turned into Round Three quickly; laughter and stories of scandalous activities filled the table. Cannon joined them for a round and impressed Captain Montpellier by finishing his tankard first.

Fontaine got an angry look on his face again as a man approached and said, "Hey are you guys doing Old Roger's Run?"

"Old Roger's Run? What's that?" Zygmunt replied.

The man set his beer down on their table oblivious to Fontaine's look and said, "Old Roger's Run is the legendary Borracho drinking quest. Participants have 12 hours to visit the Run's 12 official pubs and consume 48 drinks: 36 beers and 12 shots of spirits. The Run starts at six in the evening and ends at six in the morning. Each person has to drink three beers and do one shot of spirits at each pub."

"What do you get if you complete it?" Zygmunt said.

"Old Roger's Tankard; a large drinking vessel that's twice as large as a normal tankard. Holders of it are entitled to one free fill-up per night at any of the 12 pubs that participate in the Run. Now mind you, I only know of five people who have ever successfully completed it."

"Don't forget the final stop," Montpellier said grinning.

The man broke into a wide smile and said, "Old Stop 13. Don't complete that and you don't earn Old Roger's Tankard!"

"What's Stop 13?" Zygmunt asked.

Montpellier and the man exchanged smiles and Montpellier said, "After you've visited all 12 pubs and consumed all 48 drinks, you have to visit Ye Olde Pleasure Shack and successfully bed one of the fine ladies who works there!"

"Finest whorehouse on Borracho. The Stop 13 is the one that's foiled many a man!"

All five of them burst out laughing, even Fontaine was amused.

"Tankard's presented to you by Captain Morgan himself," the main said to Zygmunt.

"We'll have to try it sometime," he responded.

His drinking companions agreed, but not tonight. They informed the man of this and he went on his way.

"Cannon, is this pub one of the 12 that's part of Old Roger's Run?" Zygmunt asked him.

"Yes it is; proudly."

"Is there an order to the 12?"

"One can do it in any order, as long as they mention that they're participating in the Run at each pub. The one exception is that the last pub has to be The Red Wolf."

"Why?"

"Tradition Babushka; tradition's important."

Wanting to say something, but wisely opting not to, Zygmunt continued, "How does Captain Morgan know that one actually visited all 12 pubs?"

"At each pub, as well as the 13th stop, participants are handed a piece of parchment declaring that they're on the run. Each of the 13 stops has a different design, and the proprietor signs and dates it before handing it to the person. You don't get it until you've finished the four drinks. You must collect all 13 before six in the morning or you don't earn the Tankard."

"I'm going to do it one day!" Jenny interjected, followed by Alice stating the same.

"You can't do it! You're a girl," Zygmunt replied.

Jumping to her feet, Jenny made for him with both fists clenched.

"Whoa, easy!" Fontaine said, stepping in front of her. Piwoski and Montpellier also rose and helped calm the situation.

"Fuck you Babushka! I can drink you under the table anywhere, anytime!"

Zygmunt let out a laugh and rolled his eyes, "What about Stop 13?"

Jenny burst out laughing and said, "I can screw better than any of the Half-Masters on this rotten island! Not a one of them would be able to keep up! You'll see Babushka; I'll hoist that Tankard yet. I'll be drinking from it with the captain in his lagoon."

A smile of certainty rested on her face. The rest of the table nodded in approval, except for Zygmunt. Shortly after, the group finished their drinks and decided to move on. They thanked Cannon for his hospitality and headed out.

Jenny and Alice bade goodnight to the group and proceeded off on their own. The men headed back to the waterfront and arrived at the grandest pub on the island; The Red Wolf.

The pub was laid out like a pirate ship; one traveled from the bottom to the top as they moved through its three distinct sections. The front of the two-story structure featured ornately-carved wooden figures and multicolored glass windows on either side of the center door. Entering the pub, the ground floor section represented the lower section of a sailing vessel. Crates, nets, oars and other such supplies decorated the walls. Some of the wooden crates served as either seats, chairs, or both. Tables filled the 50-person room, with dark-red luxurious booths lining the wall on either side of the door, as well as the back right-side wall. A large bar with tons of massive beer barrels stood on the opposite side of the door. In the far-left corner of the room stood a staircase that led up to the second floor.

The second floor was comprised of a separate room to the right, and a hallway to the left. The room to the right was split into two distinct sections that represented a captain's cabin. The front section occupied 30 percent of the area, the rear section took up the other 70 percent. The front section had a low roof and was quite intimate. There was a shelf for customers to set their drinks on and room for about five to stand alongside it. A narrow strip of free space wide enough for two people to pass separated it from the other part of the front area, which was where the booze was. The bar in this area had six stools that faced the bartender. The main portion of the room was in the rear section and was lined with booths and tables, similar to the room on the ground floor. It could hold roughly 35 people. One massive chandelier lit the rear section, while smaller candles illuminated the dimly-lit bar area.

The true party however could always be found in the third section. From the top of the stairwell, instead of going to the captain's cabin on the right, one headed down the hallway to the left that led to the outside area. This section represented the "deck" and was always packed. A massive bar filled the area to the right of the entrance and was kept continuously busy by the more than 100 people who filled the huge, open-air room. Tall walls stood on three sides, but had large arches cut in them that let in a lot of light. There was no roof, but thick colorful cloth strips were strung along the length of the upper section of the walls, creating a "ceiling" of sorts. Every night the deck area was filled with scallywags, with neither wind nor rain keeping people away.

Making their way through the lower section, the group went upstairs and headed right to the outside deck area. Within minutes they had commanded a table, tankards of beer and four healthy wenches.

The rest of the night was spent in a whirl of drinking, storytelling, laughing and cavorting.

PAGE INTENTIONALLY LEFT BLANK

CHAPTER FOURTEEN

THE SUN HAD ALREADY PASSED its pinnacle and was halfway toward its daily demise when Captain Montpellier raised his head from the pillow. The pounding in his head was serious enough for him to warrant his raising it a mistake. Getting all the way out of bed was an even more painful experience. He looked back down at the bed, but the beautiful woman who had slid beneath the covers with him the night before was nowhere to be seen.

Stumbling into some clothes, he managed to put both legs into one pant leg and promptly fell over with a curse. Finally managing to get decently dressed, he headed downstairs, presenting an amusing sight as he pinballed from side to side going down.

Cursing the sun's rays, he threw it as nasty a glare as he could and set off in search of food. Finding a basement tavern called the Hole in the Hull, he stumbled down the stairs and was grateful for the darkened interior that existed on the other side of the wooden door.

Ordering bread, cheese and some coffee, he sat down near the back of the establishment. The tavern's walls consisted of faded orange bricks that curved around the circular room. The floor was cobblestone; timbered beams comprised most of the roof.

Two men were talking at a table in front of him, while a solitary man was at the table to his right. The more Montpellier ate, the more he felt himself coming back to life. Food works wonders on hangovers. It's tough getting it down, but it provides the fuel the body desperately needs.

Sitting back in his chair, he felt the brick wall cool against his back. Sipping a fresh mug of coffee, he tried unsuccessfully to tune out the conversation at the table in front of him.

"No, listen; *listen*. They're savages. They're not like us."

"You're wrong, they're people just like us."

"No they're not! They're apes. That's why it's totally fine that they're enslaved."

"You're crazy mate. They're as human as you and me, with families and everything."

"You don't understand; listen to me. They are made for work. That's all the negros are good for."

Montpellier cast a hard stare at the man who had just finished talking. Looking away from his companion, the man noticed Montpellier and shot him an equally nasty look.

"You have a problem!?" he said, the booze-fueled words coming out faster than normal.

Montpellier didn't say a word, but didn't break the stare either.

"I said do you have a problem!?"

"I heard what you said."

The man made a move to stand, but his companion pushed him back down.

Montpellier returned his attention to the last of his food.

"You a negro lover too?" the man spat the words at him.

"I have had the pleasure of meeting many fine black men and women in my travels, so I take firm exception to your filthy views."

The solitary man at the table to Montpellier's right let out a short, humorless laugh that caused all three to turn and look at him.

Turning his head to stare at them, the first thing they noticed were his eyes. Some have described them as crystal eyes. They were a rich brilliant blue, but sharp as the rays of the setting sun. His hair was light brown and flowed perfectly backwards before cascading down each side. The full beard was trimmed short, highlighting both care and vanity. He was medium high, though a bit on the short side. Muscular arms and a stout chest mixed with his thin frame.

In crisp, proper English, he looked at Montpellier and said, "Leave it to a Frenchman not to understand the nature of man. There is a natural order to things boy. Some races are naturally inferior."

Montpellier set his coffee down and said, "My name is Captain Jacques le Pinard Montpellier. And you are?"

"Cutter."

"Why don't you mind your own business Cutter, you miserable sack of shit."

"This is my business."

"Other people's conversations?"

"Slaves; best slaver in the Caribbean."

Montpellier's gaze hardened. The two men stared at each other silently. All activity ceased. Voices dropped to murmurs.

The corners of Cutter's lips were curled in a thin smile that oozed superiority. Montpellier broke the stare, grabbed his mug and roughly finished the coffee.

Standing up, he spat the last of it out onto the floor and said, "Makes me sick to breathe the same air as you."

"*Au revoir*," Cutter mockingly called out to the departing figure. "Montpellier," he said to himself. "What a despicable name."

After he had gone, Cutter ordered another tankard of beer and looked at the two men at the table in front of him. "You are a fool," he said to the man who had been debating his racist companion. "Negros are property, nothing more. They are here to be worked until they drop and then replaced with the next one. They exist for no other reason. Remember that word; property."

Montpellier didn't know where he was going as he walked through town. His mind was still back in the tavern with the English slaver. Walking into the Sunken Vessel, he kicked a chair at the bar to the side and quickly sat in it. The man on the other side cast him a sideways glance, but said nothing.

"You open?" Montpellier asked him.

"Just did; welcome back."

"Back?"

"You were here last night with three friends. You met Emperor Sandbar I."

Montpellier looked up at the big fish above the bar and then back at the bartender. "The crazy old guy who says he's the Emperor of the Caribbean. Right. You once killed a guy with that fish up there if I remember correctly."

"That's right. What was your name again?"

"Captain Jacques le Pinard Montpellier."

"Welcome back Captain. I'm Lucas."

"Pleasure to be in your establishment again Lucas. I could really use a beer."

"Coming right up."

Lucas joined the captain in a drink. They clinked mugs and sipped their beers.

No one was in the place but the two of them. Talk flowed freely and they traded brief versions of their past. One beer turned into three rums, and eventually the conversation worked its way back around to Emperor Sandbar I.

"I understand that he ran into horrible luck with the hurricane and all, but what was this treasure you say he was after?"

"The lost treasure of Old Havana. More of a myth than anything else. You know how it goes."

"What's the story behind it?"

Lucas finished another rum and checked the bar to ensure no one else had entered. Looking back at Montpellier, he poured them each a fresh drink and said, "Normally I never talk about it, or just brush it off as nothing since I don't want to upset the emperor. As you can imagine, it's not a topic he ever wishes to discuss. But since we're all alone, let me tell you, I believe that the treasure actually exists!"

The rum was working its magic on him and the words flowed uninhibited.

"Around 100 years ago, there was a French pirate named Jacques de Sores who sacked Old Havana in 1555. He completely destroyed the town, burned it to the ground and stole its entire treasure. The town was rebuilt of course, and sometime later he was killed."

"But the treasure…"

"That's right Captain; the treasure was never found. He never mentioned what happened to it or where he hid it. Those who knew him testified that he didn't spend it, and it wasn't found on his ship. Therefore, it must still be out there."

"You sure he didn't just spend it?"

"It's been 100 years, so I can't say for sure. But I believe it's still out there. De Sores got ambushed by the Spanish Navy and was killed after the assault. He was a shrewd man though. The attack on Old Havana was spectacular! The perfect combination of clever planning mixed with fearless execution. This wasn't some run-of-the-mill pirate who just got lucky and then spent it all on wine and women. This was someone who would have thought about what to do with all that gold once he acquired it."

"And you believe it's just sitting in the ground somewhere?"

"Most of it, yes. I have heard too many stories from too many pirates to believe that it's all just crazy talk."

Montpellier set down his beaker and looked intently at Lucas. "If you believe so strongly that this isn't just some stupid pirate tale, why haven't you set out after it yourself?"

"I came to this island to be a bar owner because I respect the pirates. They shake their fists at all of society's enforced rules and refuse to bow down to the corrupt governments in power. I came because owning a bar here is great business. I have a great life. I'm always entertained by my clients and I want for nothing. Here is paradise for me." Lucas paused and let out a long sigh before continuing, "As for the treasure, I have seen three people set off in pursuit of it and all three came back worse than they were when they set off. Seeing the emperor in here most nights is...sobering. I have all I need here; I don't want that kind of misery."

"Just because others have failed doesn't mean it's a lost cause."

"Indeed my friend. I see the twinkle in your eye that I've seen before. You sound like a rather successful pirate, why bother chasing the treasure?"

"It's not about the treasure Lucas, it's about the *adventure*! The hunt for it, that's what excites me! Now what else do you know about it? Where might one look?"

"I have warned you about what happened to those who sought it before you, but if you're serious about knowing more, seek out an old pirate named Roundhorn. He usually hangs out at either the Hog's Breath or the Rudderless Schooner. He knows more about it than anyone."

Montpellier pounded the last of his drink, wobbly got off the barstool and vigorously shook Lucas' hand. Laying down far more coins than necessary, he thanked him for his hospitality and headed out just as new customers finally were coming in.

Later that same night, Jenny and Alice were drinking in a popular tavern called Powder & Shot. The bar was in the middle of the room with tables and chairs set up both to the left and the right of it. There was a stage in the right corner that often featured lively musicians competing with the pub's resident deranged pianist. Stairs in the back led up to the tables on the balcony. Three chandeliers hung from the ceiling.

Jenny and Alice were drinking at a table near the stage, rising often to energetically dance in the small, open area in front of it. The piano was against the wall on the left. Tonight the pianist was dominating the music. One moment he was thundering away on the keys; the next he was pounding rum and hurling nonsensical comments at the guitarists onstage.

The music was above average, and their dancing put everyone else to shame. As the night wore on, multiple men attempted to dance with them only to be promptly rebuffed. Most slinked off, muttering insults that were lost in the music. A few retreated to nearby tables and watched them with growing jealousy. Few things in this world are worse than the fragile egos of weak men hiding behind bluster. Combining that with alcohol almost always leads to trouble.

As the musicians took a break, Jenny headed to the bar for fresh drinks. Two of the rebuffed men and five of their friends rapidly approached her and maneuvered between her and the bar.

"Let's go outside and get some fresh air pretty girl," one of them said as they grabbed her arms and turned for the door.

Going limp, she let them walk her three steps towards the door before dropping her head forward and then immediately hurling it backwards. The back of her head smashed into the face of the man who had spoken. The unmistakable sound of a nose shattering pierced the air. His scream was even louder.

She threw a hard kick forward and then backward, catching two of them in the balls. Screaming curses at them, she fought to free her arms.

"You fucking bitch!" one of the men in front of her yelled, cocking his fist.

Before he could throw the punch, Alice rushed up behind him and buried her knife in the side of his neck. Her banshee scream scared them as much as the sight of the blood pouring out of their dying friend's neck.

Turning to face her, one of the men kicked her in the chest. Falling backward, she was trying to get to her feet as the man came at her with a knife. He was just starting his forward motion when a pistol shot rang out and he fell dead.

Letting go of Jenny, the remaining five men turned to face two men who had come down from the balcony and were charging at them. One of them threw aside the pistol he had just fired, and they joined the fray.

Jenny and Alice fought fiercer than anyone, and with the addition of the two men who had joined the fight on their side, they quickly finished off the attackers. Two of the remaining five attackers died, while the other three fled the bar, badly beaten.

Ordering fresh drinks, Jenny, Alice and the two men headed back to the table by the piano. The two introduced themselves as Billy and Bob Boots. The ladies thanked them for their assistance and complimented them on their fighting skills.

Returning the compliment, Billy lowered his voice and said, "We're wanted men you know. The British are after us for engaging in piracy."

"Honey everyone on this island is wanted by the authorities for engaging in piracy!" Alice retorted loudly, causing those nearby to burst out laughing and raise their tankards in support of the statement.

The four of them drank long into the evening. The ladies finally bid them goodnight and departed as the hour passed four.

PAGE INTENTIONALLY LEFT BLANK

Part 5:
Nature's Fury

PAGE INTENTIONALLY LEFT BLANK

CHAPTER FIFTEEN

CAPTAIN UMBERLAND, having given his crew enough time to recover from their fight with Captain Van Muis at the Crazy Goat, finally gave the order for them to head off to plunder the Spanish town of Rojanz. With the weather on their side, he anticipated arriving in about five days.

The smaller supply ship they had purchased before heading off was renamed the *Admiral's Hat*. First Mate Wilcox was skippering it with a crew of five. After two days of sailing, both ships were running well and they were slightly ahead of schedule.

Around noon on the third day, Captain Umberland strolled to the front of the ship and approached Lightning. He was staring intently forward, oblivious to the captain's approach until he heard him say, "This is the third time today I've seen you up here staring at the sky. You seem concerned. Everything all right?"

Turning to face the captain, he looked at him with a face devoid of any humor and said, "The first time I went to sea I was 14. Like most people, I'll never forget that initial experience of being on a ship far out to sea, no land in sight for days, the hustle and bustle of life on a big ship, being awed by the majesty of the ocean."

"The first exposure to the sea is a powerful one for sure."

"Indeed. But I also remember my first voyage for another reason."

Captain Umberland cocked an eyebrow with a mixture of interest and concern.

"One night, the sky was clear and the moon was full, but there was this strange ring of light around it. Not a tight circle, more of a big one way around it, as if someone had drawn a circle in the sky. The next day, the weather was overcast and a nasty wind was blowing. That afternoon, the worst storm I've ever experienced hit us, and we barely managed to keep the ship afloat. I was certain I was going to die, certain we all were going to the bottom. The storm raged and raged relentlessly."

Captain Umberland stared at Lightning. Lightning stared back. Above them, the wind was lashing the sails. It wasn't a strong breeze in one direction, rather an odd, choppy breeze that seemed to strike the sails unevenly. Both men looked up at the unsettling thwacking sound the sails were making, and then back down at each other. The sky was completely overcast. The ship was slowing as the water turned choppy.

"There was a ring of light around the moon last night," Captain Umberland said.

"As if someone had drawn a circle in the sky," Lightning replied.

The two men stared silently at each other as the wind increased.

"Captain, we had better batten down the hatches. We had better batten them down *tight*."

Captain Umberland nodded sternly and walked briskly back across the deck as Lightning resumed staring at the sky uneasily.

The sky was completely dark two hours before the sunset. The rain started with a thud, as if a hole had opened in the clouds. The wind seemed to be as loud as it was strong. No one spoke as the cook served up what he could in the increasingly violent waters. Half the crew didn't bother trying to eat; half who did couldn't keep it down. An hour later, all holy hell was unleashed upon them.

The rain fell hard and the wind blew fierce. The waves were the worst part. The short ones would throw the boats off-center just before the larger ones slammed into them. It was as if they were working together against the two ships. It took every ounce of energy the crews had to fight the waves and remain afloat.

Aboard the *Grog Hog*, Captain Umberland stood on the Quarterdeck and watched the incoming waves, shouting orders to Jenkins who was gripping the helm with all his might. Below him, the crew worked frantically to keep the sails and rigging secure, while also continuously bailing out the water accumulating on the deck.

"Hard to Starboard!" Captain Umberland yelled as he saw the dark mass of the next wave rising to his right.

Jenkins, his hands already bloodied and practically numb, cursed in exertion as he spun the heavy wooden wheel. His arms ached, his legs burned, and pain shot up and down his back.

The ship swung to face the oncoming wave, getting just close enough into position to ride over it, yet not enough to avoid another huge blast of water hurling across the deck.

"Floaters! Floaters!" Captain Umberland screamed after watching two men get swept over the side and into the furious waters. He closed his eyes for a second as the crew tossed floatable objects overboard. The two were already obscured from view by the time they hit the water. All knew the pair didn't stand a chance, but they tossed the floaters in anyway.

The crew was a family and they would do everything possible to save some of their own. Who knows; maybe a miracle would save the two doomed men thrashing amongst the hellish waves. But no miracle awaited them, only a death as horrible as it was inevitable.

Like a battle, one of the cruelest elements of the storm was that it showed no sympathy, provided no time for reflection or mourning of the fallen. Almost the instant the floaters hit the water, the storm's fury demanded all to return to their posts, forcing them to think of those lost no more, lest they share their fate.

For all the attention Captain Umberland put towards keeping the ship afloat, he couldn't push his concern for the *Admiral's Hat* out of his mind. If the *Grog Hog* was struggling this much to stay afloat, how must the smaller vessel be faring?

Over on the *Admiral's Hat*, Wilcox and his small crew were fighting for their lives. Each wave was harder and harder to recover from, and the amount of water that had accumulated on deck made it more difficult to steer, as well as to stay afloat.

Wilcox could barely see the *Grog Hog* in front of him. Each wave seemed larger than the last and hit with greater force.

"Brace yourselves!" he screamed as a smaller wave grew in size just as it reached them. The men gripped whatever they could and pushed their heads against their chests. The powerful rush of water thundered over them. The men mustered all their strength to hold on. The ship tossed about like a toy in a bathtub.

"We can't last in this!" one of the men shouted as they desperately maneuvered the ship to survive the next assault.

"What do we do Cap'n!?" the man valiantly working the helm yelled at Wilcox.

Through the darkness, a flash of lightning enabled Wilcox to spot the *Grog Hog,* cresting a wave ahead of them. As suddenly as the illumination had appeared, it disappeared. Total darkness enveloped them again.

"Make for the *Grog Hog!*" Wilcox yelled to the helmsman. "Owens, raise the Committee Flag!"

"Aye!" both men yelled over the wind. The helmsman heaved the wheel, while Owens stumbled below deck to search for the bright orange flag that they used to signal each other to join up.

Owens cursed as he was slammed from side to side in the dark. Tossing food, clothing and guns aside, he screamed as the ship lurched down a wave, sending him crashing into the side of the ship. Bursting back onto the deck, he shouted, "I can't find it Cap'n!" A torrent of water enveloped the deck a second later.

"What!?" Wilcox yelled at him.

"I can't find the bloody flag! The conditions are too bad!"

"You either find that flag or we're dead!"

Owens desperately glanced at the stairs leading below deck and then back at Wilcox.

"Wave breaking! Port side!" one of the men screamed. Everyone braced themselves as best as they could as the ship struggled to meet the oncoming wave.

They all spat out water once the wave finished passing over them. Wilcox sprung to his feet and screamed at Owens, "Get back down there and find that flag, or I'll end you! NOW!"

Owens, now as scared of Wilcox as he was of the storm, shouted "Aye Cap'n!", and scrambled below deck.

Two medium-sized waves crashed upon the ship. They fared well on the first one, but the second hit harder and caught them out of position.

As the second wave was about to hit, Owens appeared back on deck holding the Committee Flag shouting, "I found it!"

The second wave passing over them was accompanied by a monstrous cracking sound. Wilcox's heart sank as he watched the mast snap and topple overboard. The water from the wave began to overwhelm the ship and a significant list developed almost immediately.

"Cap'n! Help!" a voiced cried out from the port side. Stumbling across the deck, Wilcox spotted Owens hanging over the rail, his feet dragging in the sea. Pulling him back over, the two fell in a heap onto the deck.

"It's gone Cap'n," Owens said despondently. "I lost the Committee Flag. Just couldn't hold onto it."

"You did well Owens. It doesn't matter anymore anyway," Wilcox replied, gesturing towards the broken mast.

"Cap'n! I can't steer her!" the helmsman shouted from the wheel.

Wilcox looked over the crippled ship. Ahead of them, a flash of lightning illuminated the *Grog Hog* cresting another wave. "God damn you Umberland. God damn you to Hell. You have killed us all you bastard," he hissed through clenched teeth as they watched a wave rise up to their right.

The wave charged forward like a bull.

"This is it lads!" Wilcox shouted. "Toss all the floaters overboard! Every man for himself!"

The men threw the floaters over both sides of the ship and then reached for anything to hold onto. Terror filled their eyes as the wave broke upon them like a demon from an ancient tale.

The ship buckled under the weight and force of the water, and with a horrendous sound, succumbed to the storm's fury. The men onboard were washed into the churning waters to meet the fate that awaited them.

Onboard the *Grog Hog*, Captain Umberland had been periodically turning his spyglass back to check on the *Admiral's Hat*. The smaller ship had done an amazing job keeping up in the storm and he was proud of her crew, especially Wilcox.

The last time he checked on them, they appeared to be struggling more than before. Now as he scanned the dark waters, his concern grew. He could find no trace of them.

A wave smashed into them and the entire ship lurched from the impact. Water rushed across the deck, spreading havoc in its wake. Crates broke loose and sprang apart, further complicating the crew's efforts at maintaining order.

For a spell, Captain Umberland's attention was fully occupied with conditions aboard the *Grog Hog*. As soon as the slightest break allowed, he swung his spyglass back towards the last place he had seen the *Admiral's Hat*.

No matter how hard he looked, no sign of them could be found. A lightning strike briefly illuminated a distant wave and for a split second, he thought he saw a large piece of wood floating in it. Darkness immediately obscured all again. The rain fell relentlessly.

"Lightning! Come up here now!" he shouted down to the deck.

Struggling up the slick stairs, Lightning was almost thrown over the side when another wave struck.

"Captain!" he shouted upon reaching the Quarterdeck.

"No sign of the *Admiral's Hat*," Captain Umberland said, shoving the spyglass into his hand. "You have younger eyes. See if you can spot them."

Lightning stumbled to the stern and raised the spyglass. The rain played havoc with visibility and the lurching deck made standing quite the challenge. Despite these obstacles, Lightning valiantly scanned the waters for any sign of their endangered mates.

"Anything?" Captain Umberland shouted at him. "Lightning? Lightning!"

Lightning jerked his head around and looked at Captain Umberland, who held out his hands, palms-up questioningly. Lightning lowered the spyglass and shook his head.

Captain Umberland's face grew even more serious as Lightning made his way back and handed him the spyglass. They shared a look of mutual concern, the unspoken conclusion of their fruitless search visible in their eyes.

The sound of breaking wood jerked their attention back to the situation on their own vessel. One of the smaller masts was sagging, damaged, but not destroyed. Ropes, pulleys and cloth ripped as crew members rushed to try and stabilize it.

Lightning looked at Captain Umberland, who simply replied, "Go."

For three more long hours, the storm raged against them, pushing the crew beyond the point of exhaustion as they battled to stay afloat. They almost didn't believe it when the first rays of the dawn's light pierced the clouds, and the rain finally subsided.

The *Admiral's Hat* was lost. Two of the *Grog Hog's* crew were dead. But miraculously, everyone else was alive. Most were nursing some wound or the other, but only one of them was seriously injured. They stumbled below deck and collapsed into their bunks, to sleep like never before.

CHAPTER SIXTEEN

THE *Grog Hog* limped into the port of St. Bartholomew. Captain Umberland gave the crew two days to do as they pleased, but instructed them to stay close to the dock, as they were in an unfamiliar town.

Fortunately the ship was repairable. Yet for now, they were stuck in an unknown location and their money was running low. Once it was fixed, they would need to do some raiding to secure a new support vessel for their assault on Rojanz. That was a problem for another day however.

As St. Bartholomew's governor strolled the street that ran parallel to the dock, he greeted a few people and then paid his weekly visit to the port's tax collector.

"Morning James," he called out as he entered the small, one-story structure.

"Good morning Governor," the man replied, rising to shake his hand.

"How goes it?"

"Well Sir. How are you today?"

"Magnificent. How's business been?"

"Pretty slow Sir. Just a few merchant ships this week."

The governor nodded and reviewed the ledger that listed the arrivals.

"The one exception is a vessel that limped in here yesterday all banged up from the hurricane. The ship's called the *Grog Hog*."

"*Grog Hog* eh? Strange name for a merchant ship."

"That's what they claim they are, but…"

"But what?"

"The ship has a lot of cannons for a merchant ship. And some of her crew looked rather unsavory."

"Is she still here?"

"Yes Sir. She's being repaired now. Would you like to see her?"

"Yes I would."

"Very good Sir, I'll take you to her now."

Onboard the ship, Captain Umberland sat in his cabin listening to the sounds of repairs. He was thinking of Wilcox and wondering if he could have done anything different to save him and the other men onboard the *Admiral's Hat*. The sound of approaching voices shook him from his thoughts.

"Hello there!" a man shouted from the pier.

Captain Umberland left his cabin and walked up on deck. "Hello," he called over to the two men. He recognized the man on the left as the town's dock manager. He had a feeling the man didn't like them and that this was not a social visit.

"I'm Governor Maxwell. Looks like you had some trouble out there in the storm."

"Yes we did. Nastier storm than we've ever encountered before."

"May we come aboard?"

"Of course Governor, please."

The two men boarded and shook hands with him.

"So what happened?" Governor Maxwell asked.

Captain Umberland described the storm and the damage they sustained in it, as well as the two crew members who were swept overboard. He left out the part regarding the *Admiral's Hat*, as they had already discreetly inquired about it, only to be informed that no ship matching its description had arrived recently. He also didn't mention the severely wounded crew member, as Jacob had informed him that the man was awake, but dying.

Governor Maxwell nodded his head repeatedly, but Captain Umberland noticed that his eyes moved constantly around the ship.

When he finished talking, the Governor replied, "Horrible storm. Very sorry to hear about your losses."

"Thank you Governor."

"I'm curious Captain… you are merchants, correct?"

"That's correct Sir."

"What merchandise are you currently carrying?"

"We deal in cocoa beans and rum. We don't currently have merchandise onboard. We're on our way to Columbia to purchase goods to sell in New England."

The governor nodded again and told Captain Umberland to enjoy his stay on St. Bartholomew. Captain Umberland thanked him for the visit. As he watched the two men walk away, he had an uneasy feeling about their visit. Turning to the crew members repairing the ship, he urged them to work faster and then retired back to his cabin.

Elsewhere in town, four of the *Grog Hog's* crew were drinking in a tavern away from the bustle of the dock. The men occupied two tables and were sharing a bottle of rum along with each man's tankard of beer. The conversation had begun civilly enough, but the mood changed quickly.

"Wrong! He could have done something!" Dogfish said, pounding the table.

"What? What could the captain have done?" Adam responded. "If he had tried to turn the ship around in those waves, we all would be dining with Davy Jones right now!"

"No we wouldn't be! He just sailed on and let them fellas on the *Admiral's Hat* drown!"

"Dogfish is right. Cap'n abandoned them! Just plain *abandoned* them!" Scrag said, taking a pull from his tankard and letting the foam settle on his large, unkempt beard. "He only cares about himself, not us. Not *any* of us!"

"Right! He only cares about himself, the selfish bastard!" Dogfish said, pointing admirably at Scrag.

"If he did it to them, he'll do it to us. *Any* of us!" Scrag said, looking hard at Adam.

"The captain was put in a tough spot. No one could have known how nasty that storm was," Adam responded, matching Scrag's look. "Sure it was a little heartless to sail on, but he had no other choice! He had to think of the rest of us."

"He was only thinking of himself!" Scrag snapped back.

"A little heartless!? It was an outright betrayal! A crime!" Dogfish shouted.

"So what do we do?" Java interjected. "Just forget it and move on?"

"We'll forget nothing," Dogfish hissed.

"Well then, what? What do we do?" Java inquired again.

Just then, the tavern door swung open and four ladies strolled in. The conversation at the table subsided immediately as the four men observed the ladies heading to the bar. Grabbing fresh tankards, they walked over to the pirates and set the beers on the table, their outfits accentuating their assets.

"Compliments of the proprietor," the lady in the bright pink corset said, looking directly at Dogfish.

"Thanks," Dogfish said, quickly standing up, scratching the chair legs against the floor in his haste. "I'm Dogfish. They call me that 'cause I'm strong like a dog."

"And ugly like a fish!" Scrag interjected, grinning broadly.

"Look who's talkin'!" Dogfish snapped at him. "You look like a deranged woodpecker mistook your face for a tree!"

"Well some women like a man who is strong as a dog," the lady in the pink corset said, resting her hand on Dogfish's arm.

The smile spread quickly across Dogfish's face as the lady introduced herself as Rose and sat down next to him. The other three ladies introduced themselves and took a seat next to each of the other three.

In good time, the eight of them were loudly laughing and then retired to rooms in the building next door.

After they had departed, the tavern's owner chuckled and said to the sole remaining customer, "Little trick I learned a long time ago. If the fellas start getting rowdy, call in Rose and the girls; works every time."

The customer nodded and went back to his solitary drinking.

CHAPTER SEVENTEEN

AFTER FOUR DAYS of continual repairs, the *Grog Hog* was once again ready to put to sea. Captain Umberland sent out word for the crew to return to the ship, as he wanted them to sleep onboard that night, so they could leave first thing in the morning. He greeted each as they arrived back.

"Welcome back Dogfish, Adam, Scrag, Java," he said as the four men stepped aboard.

"No one left behind this time, eh Cap'n?" Dogfish said.

"This time?"

"It's good to be back onboard Cap'n," Dogfish replied and headed below, followed by the other three.

The last of the pirates made it back to the ship as the sun provided its final illumination. Captain Umberland was on deck examining the repair work of the damaged mast and trying to determine if they had enough supplies to attempt a fresh try for Rojanz, or if they needed to wait and secure additional resources.

His thoughts were interrupted by Sam shouting from the Quarterdeck, "Captain!"

There was an unsettling urgency in his voice and Captain Umberland hurried up to meet him. Sam didn't say a word when he arrived, he just pointed. Following his direction, Captain Umberland instantly spotted the source of the urgency. Sailing through the harbor entrance was a British warship.

"Shit!" Captain Umberland said. Sam nodded gloomily.

"All hands on deck!" Captain Umberland shouted, racing down to the deck as men scrambled up to join him.

"What's going on Cap'n?" Barrel asked, spotting the concern on his face.

"English warship sailing into the harbor. We need to leave immediately. Everyone to your battle stations. Show no mercy!"

"Sorry Captain, but that's not possible right now," Jenkins said, his words freezing everyone. "It's low tide. We can't maneuver at all."

Captain Umberland glared at Jenkins and said, "Get your ass over to that wheel and do what you can!"

"Aye Captain!"

"We'll never survive an assault by a warship if we can't maneuver Captain!" Dogfish said. "We should surrender."

"Surrender!?" Barrel shouted, shooting him a look of pure disgust.

"It's the only way," Scrag said. "They'll kill us otherwise."

"They'll kill us if we surrender!" Lightning snapped at him.

"You don't know that!" Dogfish shouted.

"What do you think happens to pirates who surrender!?" Lightning retorted.

"Silence!" Captain Umberland said, slamming his hand down on the railing.

The deck fell quiet. Tension enveloped the group like fog swallowing a city street.

"Captain! They appear to have stopped!" Jenkins called out from the helm.

Captain Umberland raced up to the Quarterdeck and looked through his spyglass. Sure enough, the warship had stopped a little inside the harbor's entrance.

"Low tide," he said, lowering his spyglass.

"They won't be able to maneuver either," Jenkins replied.

Captain Umberland nodded and raised his spyglass again, scanned the harbor intently. After a minute, he heard Jenkins say, "They'll not be able to move on us until the tide rises, about 10 hours I reckon. Probably hit us at first light."

Hearing no response from him, Jenkins continued, "Not to be negative Captain, but this isn't that big of a harbor. They have position on us and they can remain, while we have to get out. It's possible to win, but we have a lot stacked against us."

"Looks like a pretty formidable vessel too Jenkins. It'll be one hell of a fight tomorrow."

Captain Umberland walked down to the deck and faced the men. He stared at them silently for a bit and then said, "Looks like the bastards are holding up near the entrance for the night. They'll attack as soon as the tide allows, probably around sunrise. Sam, Barrel, Lightning, Parrot; stand guard and watch that ship hard. Jenkins, stay at the helm for now. The rest of you, head below and get some chow. I'll call for five of you to relieve the watch in a few hours."

The men nodded silently and moved off in various directions.

The hour was approaching midnight when Captain Umberland emerged from his cabin and walked on deck. He checked with each of the four new men standing watch and then headed up to the Quarterdeck.

"I told you to get some chow about two hours ago," he said to Jenkins. "Where's the man I sent to relieve you?"

"I told him to get some chow."

"When was that?"

"About two hours ago."

Both men stared at each other for a second and then started laughing.

"Fine," Captain Umberland said. "Don't go get some chow."

"Aye Captain."

Captain Umberland smiled and shook his head. Staring at the English ship through his spyglass he said, "Well, they haven't surrendered yet."

Jenkins chuckled and said, "No Captain, not yet."

"Hmm..." Captain Umberland murmured as he stared through his spyglass. "It appears that they're towing a small vessel behind them."

"I noticed that earlier. I spotted a few people on it, but they didn't appear to be soldiers. It looks like they helped save a small ship and towed it with them here. You can see some damage on the deck, but the mast and rigging still look operational."

Umberland scanned the rear of the warship and then down the connecting lines to the smaller vessel. He watched as four people emerged from below and paced its deck. They were clearly not soldiers.

"Pretty dark tonight, eh Jenkins?"

"Aye Captain. No moon."

"No moon..."

"Jenkins," Captain Umberland said suddenly, snapping the spyglass shut and turning to face him. "I have a mission for you."

The night sky had just lost its battle against the coming dawn when the English warship *HMS Triumph* began to move. Captain Hampton gave orders for the small vessel they had towed with them to be cut free, so they could engage the pirate ship trapped in the harbor.

Lieutenant Rogers forwarded the order to two of the sailors who promptly walked to the stern with their knives.

"Sir! She's not there!" one of them called out upon reaching the back of the ship.

Lieutenant Rogers and Captain Hampton raced over to them and stared down at the cut lines that had been securing the smaller ship.

"Captain, look!" said one of the men, pointing past the harbor entrance.

Raising his spyglass, Captain Hampton spotted five people in a rowboat, rowing towards them. Staring intently, he recognized one of them as the captain of the small vessel they had rescued the day before.

He closed his eyes for a second and clenched his teeth in anger. Gripping the railing furiously, he barked orders for the ship to head to sea in pursuit of the pirates.

CHAPTER EIGHTEEN

By popular vote, the crew sailing under Captain Umberland named the small ship they had stolen, *Victory*. They sailed her as fast as she would go, knowing that the English would be relentlessly pursing them now that the sun has risen.

At the bow, two men stood watch, scanning the horizon for any sign of a larger ship to conquer. At the stern, two men looked back for any sign of the *HMS Triumph*.

Morning turned to afternoon.

"Sails Captain! Sails!" one of the men at the bow shouted, gesturing to the right.

"Jenkins, 20 degrees to starboard!" Captain Umberland said. "The rest of you, head below until I give the word."

"It's very cramped down there Captain," Joseph replied. "Can't I stay here on deck?"

"No Joseph, I need you down with the others."

Joseph nodded and headed down the short staircase.

The pirates crowded below as Jenkins steered them towards the distant ship.

"Lightning, get up here!" Captain Umberland yelled down the stairs.

"Whatcha need?" Lightning said, scrambling topside.

"We need a flag quickly."

"What flag Captain?"

"Look below and see if you can find anything we can use."

Lightning headed below and suddenly shouted, "Oh God! What is that!?"

A foul stench filled the cramped quarters and almost made his eyes water. The rest of the crew had pushed as far away from Joseph as they could, whose protests of innocence were interrupted by yet another massive fart.

"Fucking Joseph!" Lightning yelled, trying his best to find a suitable cloth to use.

"Lightning, hurry!" Captain Umberland shouted.

"I'm trying Captain! I can't bloody breathe down here due to Joseph and his farts!"

"I told the captain I wanted to stay on deck," Joseph protested, ripping off yet another blast, followed by further cries of pain from the rest of the crew.

Lightning snatched a two-colored cloth out of a chest and raced for the stairs. Shouts of "take us with you" accompanied him as he lunged onto the deck, coughing repeatedly.

"Will this work Captain?" he asked, holding up the cloth.

"It'll have to. We're closing in on them. Get it up there."

Lightning hustled up the mast as quickly as he could and attached the cloth to the top.

When he got back down, he was told to stay on deck.

"No argument here!" he retorted with a huge grin that Captain Umberland found puzzling. "Don't ask," was all he offered, casting a distasteful look at the stairs leading below.

As *Victory* sailed up close to the larger ship, several people stood at the railing looking down at them. Captain Umberland could feel their apprehension.

"Good afternoon!" he called out to them jovially.

A man elbowed his way to the railing and curtly responded, "Good afternoon. I'm captain of this vessel. What's your business?"

Captain Umberland tapped the deck three times with his foot and said, "*You're* the captain of that ship?"

"Yes," the man replied annoyed. "I'm the captain."

"WRONG!" Lightning shouted, pulling out his sword right as the rest of the crew burst from below deck, yelling as loudly as they could.

The people on the other ship retreated in horror but didn't even have time to panic. Seeing the pirates secure hooks, climb up and board the vessel, they knew they were conquered. Throwing their hands in the air, they begged for mercy from the screaming horde on all sides.

"Lads! We're back in business!" Captain Umberland shouted as he stood in front of them smiling broadly.

They responded with a roar of good cheer; all were in high spirits again.

They set the passengers of the conquered ship into its lifeboats and told them that an English warship would soon be along to rescue them.

Lightning and four others manned the smaller ship, while Captain Umberland and the rest of the crew stayed on the newly taken ship. Both ships turned hard to port and sailed rapidly east, aided by a generous headwind. All felt that their luck had turned at last.

As darkness enveloped the two ships, Captain Umberland ordered the smaller vessel to come alongside. Attaching it to the back of the larger ship, he had the five men onboard her come over so all could be present at the victory feast. The two cooks prepared the best food they could find, and the wine flowed freely.

After all had consumed a fair share of food and downed multiple mugs of wine, Captain Umberland stood up and called for attention. Gripping his drink, he smiled broadly and said, "Lads we did it! We're survivors! First came the hellish storm that tragically claimed five of our own. Then we found ourselves trapped like rats in the harbor by the Royal Navy with certain death only hours away. But yet again we survived!"

All roared mightily in approval; aided by the wine of course.

Slapping Lightning on the shoulder, he continued, "Now we have a new ship and will proceed with double the resolve!"

"Are we still heading to Rojanz Captain?" Dogfish called out.

"Yes we are! First however, we need to stop somewhere and get more weapons."

"Where are we now?" Scrag asked.

"Based on what they said in that shithole town we almost died in yesterday, it sounds like we're in the southern portion of the Caribbean. Rojanz should be about a five-day sail away, once we actually head for her. This ship is stocked full and was coming from the west, so there should be a port close by. Jenkins, tomorrow morning head us due west."

"Aye Cap'n."

Finishing his wine in one go and refilling the mug, Captain Umberland looked around at the men gathered with him and continued, "We need a new first mate, and a new name for this lovely vessel that is now our home. Let's start by choosing the new name."

"How about *Victory?*" Joseph called out, spilling his wine in the process.

"*Victory* is a good name," Parrot chimed in.

"The smaller vessel's already named that," Sam said.

"So? They can both be called it!" Joseph responded.

Laughter filled the air as Captain Umberland smiled and said, "Oh Joseph."

"How about the *Plowing Bow?*" Lightning said grinning.

"Sounds like being in the sack with a wench," Sam said.

"Yeah!" Lightning responded, grinning even bigger.

Captain Umberland shook his head at him and said, "No."

"Why not!? We're pirates!"

"No," Captain Umberland repeated, then passed him a bottle of wine and said, "Here, drink this!"

"How about *Death's Door?*" Barrel said.

Several turned and looked at him as Captain Umberland responded, "Interesting...why?"

"Because when you see us, you're at death's door. What you do in that moment—surrender or fight—determines whether you walk through it or not. The name symbolizes that we can't be defeated; your *only* options are to give up or die. Victory for you is not possible. We are the best. Invincible!"

Cheers broke out and many pounded their mugs approvingly on the tables in front of them.

"Plus, we were at death's door ourselves when we captured this ship. But we survived!"

The cheers rose even higher, and the wine bottles shook on the tables from the pounding.

"Let's vote!" Captain Umberland yelled. "All in favor of *Death's Door*, say 'aye.'"

A chorus of "Aye!" rang out from practically everyone.

"It's settled then! This ship is now officially named *Death's Door*. Raise 'em up!"

All held up their mugs of wine and repeated his shout, "To *Death's Door!*"

The tables absorbed the blows of the mugs as they pounded against them, were emptied, and then forcefully set back down.

"To Barrel!" someone shouted, followed by more cheers and drinking.

"I still like the *Plowing Bow* better," Lightning muttered mostly to himself.

"Quiet down lads. There's still the other order of business to be worked out," Captain Umberland said after a few minutes.

Order was restored, and all turned their attention back to him.

"We need a new first mate," he said. "I'm going to head up on deck while you all vote for who it'll be. Someone come get me once you've decided."

The sky was dark and the absence of moonlight made the stars even brighter than normal. Captain Umberland stared up at them with the same wonder that he'd had on his first night at sea, when they had shone brighter than anything he had ever seen before.

"We made it," he said to himself. "We survived."

The gentleness of the night, and the quietness of the moment, brought his thoughts back to that horrible night when they got caught in the storm. He found himself thinking of the last time he had seen Wilcox and the other four men, all fighting valiantly to keep their little ship afloat amidst the horrific waves.

A sadness suddenly came over him, and his joy at having survived was replaced by a heaviness in his heart. He and Wilcox hadn't always been the closest of friends, but he was reliable, capable, smart and brave. Men like him didn't come around every day. He didn't know the other four that well, but there were good pirates and would be missed.

Still, this was the life they had chosen. Every member of the crew had always said that they would rather die having lived briefly as masters of their own destinies, rather than lived long lives spent miserably toiling away at a job they hated in a stifling society.

Pulling his eyes away from the waves below, he looked up at the stars again. Raising his mug high he said, "Here's to you lads; to all five of you. You lived free and died as men. Here's to you!"

He finished his mug in one go and threw it overboard. He then grabbed the bottle and poured a little wine into the water below. "One last drink together old Wilcox," he said and took a pull from it.

The smile returned to his face and he felt his spirits improving. Looking out at the beautiful night sky, he gripped the handle of his sword and said, "We'll take Rojanz for you lads!"

"Captain, we have reached a decision and...what are you doing?" Lightning said, walking onto the deck and seeing him staring at the stars while gripping his sword's handle.

Captain Umberland let go of his sword, turned to him and said, "Enjoying being alive and making solemn oaths."

Lightning looked at him quizzically.

"Never mind. You've reached a decision?"

"Aye Captain."

"Good, let's go rejoin the group."

Lightning gave him a sideways glance as they headed down the stairs. "Shut up," Captain Umberland said in response. Lightning's only reply was to let out a short laugh.

"All right lads, who did you choose?" he said once he was back in his chair.

"That magnificent rogue at the end of the table," Lightning said, gesturing with his mug.

Captain Umberland stood up, walked to the other side of the table and threw an arm around Barrel's shoulder. "Congratulations to our new first mate!" he said. "Three cheers lads!"

All raised their mugs in the air and shouted, "Huzzah!" three times.

As the night was heading towards the dawn, Sam, Lightning, Parrot and Joseph bid goodnight to those remaining and stumbled off to find a place to sleep.

"Damn waves, they make it so hard to walk," Sam slurred as he stumbled from side to side down the hallway.

The other three broke out in uproariously drunken laughter and Lightning shouted out, "There are no waves tonight! It's calm as can be!"

"Yeah it's calm as can be; see!" Parrot shouted, breaking into a fast walk. He had only taken three steps when he suddenly veered hard to the left, crashed straight into the wall and fell down in a heap.

The other three exploded in laughter and awkwardly moved past him, leaving Parrot to sleep where he fell.

Settling into a bunk, Sam fell instantly to sleep. A few minutes later he woke up to find a steady stream of liquid hitting his head. Thinking he must be dreaming, he rolled over and faced the direction of the liquid.

"Ahhhhh!" he screamed as he opened his eyes to the sight of Joseph pissing on him. "Joseph!" he yelled, jumping up and throwing off the jacket that he had been using as a blanket.

Joseph mumbled inaudibly and walked back to where he had chosen to sleep, still pissing away. Screams and curses followed in his wake from those he passed.

"You're going to get it now!" Sam yelled, taking off after him. Others nearby grabbed him and drunkenly calmed him down.

And thus concluded the first night onboard the new pirate ship *Death's Door*.

CHAPTER NINETEEN

"How does your head feel First Mate Barrel?" Captain Umberland said as the two men sat in his cabin.

"Probably about as good as yours."

Captain Umberland laughed gingerly and said, "Oh well. The ship got a proper name, was christened in style and we got a new first mate."

"Indeed."

Both men sat nursing their pounding heads and sipping tea.

"So Cap'n…now do we head for Rojanz?"

"Yep, after we get more weapons and gunpowder."

"Jenkins is steering us towards where he thinks a port is."

"We'll find one. Thankfully this still looks like a respectable vessel, so we should be able to sail into any port without raising much of an alarm."

"Yep. The only thing not respectable about it is the crew!"

"Very true."

"However, let's not forget about that warship we eluded. I bet they're still searching for us."

"Guaranteed. Hmmm...I wonder if we should part ways with *Victory*."

"Probably a good idea. That's what they're looking for, unless they've already found the survivors of this ship."

Captain Umberland nodded and instructed Barrel to transfer everything on it to the *Death's Door* and then gather the crew on deck.

A few hours later, the crew assembled on the deck. Next to them stood the empty little ship. Captain Umberland pulled Barrel aside and muttered, "It took this long to transfer the supplies?"

"Well, some of the lads are moving a little slower today than most days."

"Some of them?"

"All of them I reckon. Damn it's bright today."

Captain Umberland grimaced and nodded. Then he faced the assembled men and said, "Lads, the little ship *Victory* holds a special place in our hearts. She's the ship that saved us all. Without her, we probably all would have already breathed our last."

The men began to shift their stances and cast their eyes in various directions, many already sensing what was about to happen.

Captain Umberland paced back and forth as he continued. "However, the English warship that we eluded is still out there pursuing us. And unfortunately, the brave little ship that transported us to safety is now more of a liability than an asset."

There were a few grumbles and a head shake or two, but no one actually said anything.

The captain stopped pacing and stood right in front of the men. "All right lads; step forward and take one last look at her before we do what has to be done."

Slowly and with reluctance, the men shuffled up to the railing and bade farewell to the vessel that had carried them away from almost certain death.

"All right Captain, it's time," Barrel said as the last of the men walked away.

Stepping onto the ship, they went below deck and packed some power against the port side wall. Then they lit slow-burning matches and ran back onto the *Death's Door*. Cutting the lines that connected them, the larger vessel turned hard to starboard and began sailing away.

The entire crew gathered on the deck and looked at *Victory* bobbing gently in the water. The explosion sent water and fire erupting from her port side, and she began to list. As water rushed in, the list worsened and the ship leaned way over as if trying to pick something up.

With a crack and a hiss, the ship finally succumbed to the sea's eternal embrace and slowly drifted down to join all those who had fallen before her.

Some of the pirates removed their caps. Some averted their eyes at the final moment. A sad silence filled the deck.

"Jenkins, find us a port," Captain Umberland called out as the crew dispersed to complete various tasks.

The rest of the day and night passed uneventfully. The next morning, they obtained information from a fishing vessel about where to head for supplies. A few hours later, they sailed into the port town of Elisabethville.

Ordering most of the crew to stay onboard, Umberland assigned five to stay on deck and look respectable. He reminded them that they were just here to obtain supplies and then depart. Attention was the last thing they needed.

Heading into town, he was directed to the armory. There he purchased lots of powder and shot, but unfortunately they only had a few cannons. Upon completing the transaction, he and the crew members with him began the task of transporting the items back to the ship.

Part 6: Paying For Past Sins

PAGE INTENTIONALLY LEFT BLANK

CHAPTER TWENTY

Captain Estevez boarded the *Buena Vista* and headed into his cabin, his thoughts preoccupied by the news that someone was hunting them. He knew who had sent the individual after them. He knew she would never stop hunting them. The mercenary had to be destroyed and then they had to take the fight back to the Old Country. Otherwise they would never spend another night in peace. They would never be able to stop looking over their shoulders until she was dealt with.

As the last of the crew boarded, Estevez came up on deck and called out to the helmsman Hierro Manos, "Set us on a southerly course and bounce us from island to island. I want to be near land as much as possible."

"*Si* Captain. I don't like the clouds ahead. Looks to be a rough night."

Estevez agreed and headed up to the bow of the ship.

"Always a bit sad leaving Santa Muerte," Sausalito said upon reaching Estevez at the bow about 30 minutes after they had departed.

Estevez nodded, his eyes focusing on the growing clouds overhead. He could often be found at the bow, unusual for a captain.

"How long are we going to sail south Captain?"

"Not sure. Let's keep going for three days and see if we can find the bastard, or at least hear word of him. If there is nothing, we'll reconsider our course."

The small island nicknamed "The Chipped Tooth" came into view on the left. It was so named because of the large cut that time had removed from a third of its right side.

Passing the island, the *Buena Vista* headed south.

"Sails!" Plato screamed down from the Crow's Nest, pointing behind the ship.

Javier rushed to the stern just as the other ship emerged from behind the island. It had sails out full and was roaring towards them. His eyes opened wide as the ship pushed up towards their port side, the doors of her gun ports already open.

"Gunners to your cannons!" he screamed as Captain Estevez and Sausalito ran across the deck towards him. "Captain! Her cannons are already out and she's moving fast!"

Barking orders to the crew, Estevez bounded up the stairs to the Quarterdeck while Sausalito headed below to gather their weapons.

The ship's opening salvo took out six of the *Buena Vista's* cannons and killed four.

The pirates managed to regroup and get off a round at the attackers before they could reload. The two ships furiously exchanged cannon fire for a few minutes while up top, the crews traded musket fire across the decks.

"Hard to starboard!" Estevez shouted to Hierro Manos.

The *Buena Vista* broke off the engagement and turned sharply to the right. She was damaged and had fared worse in the fight. The attacking ship was caught slightly off guard by the move, but quickly swung in pursuit of her. At the same moment, the clouds that had been gathering all day finally unleashed their rain upon them. The two ships sailed full speed into the storm.

"They're gaining on us Captain," Javier said from the stern.

Taking the spyglass from him, Estevez peered through it and saw the vessel was indeed closer than before. The pursuing ship rose on a wave and Estevez was able to spot a figure on the bow looking at him through a spyglass of his own.

"So *that's* our mysterious friend," he said to himself.

Handing Javier the spyglass, he headed down to meet Sausalito on the Quarterdeck.

"Captain we've got two teams working to repair the front ropes, they should be done soon. We'll be able to pick up a bit more speed once they're finished. I thought that bastard was supposed to be in front of us?"

"So did I; apparently things changed. Let me know the second the rigging is fixed!"

The wind had picked up and both ships were struggling with the waves and the drenching rain.

"Captain!" Sausalito shouted a short time later, running across the deck and standing at the base of the stairs to the Quarterdeck.

"What news?"

"Ropes have been repaired! Full sails?"

"No. Come up here, now!"

Joining him on the Quarterdeck, the two conferred with Hierro Manos. Javier left the stern and joined them. As they were talking, the rain softened a bit.

"Damn risky Captain," Javier said. After a second, he followed with, "That's why I like it!"

"Damn right! Let's do it!" said Hierro.

Sausalito shook his head slightly. Seeing it, Estevez broke into a wide grin and said, "Now I'm *sure* it's the right move! Let's do it just to show Sausalito what living's all about!"

"You're crazy," Sausalito said to the grinning Estevez. "But that's why I love you! I don't like this one, but you're the Captain. We follow you to the end, no matter what!"

"Love you too, you adventure-less bastard! You each know the orders to give. Weather's easing a bit. Now's the time to do it!"

The four of them broke apart. Hierro went back to the helm, Estevez went to the stern with the spyglass, Javier gathered men on the deck for instructions, and Sausalito headed below deck to the cannons.

Onboard the pursuing ship, the captain screamed at his crew to increase speed. Once he was informed that they were going as fast as possible, he placed his hand on his pistol and informed the first mate that he was convinced more speed could be obtained.

Raising the spyglass to his eye, the captain observed the *Buena Vista* ahead. The distance was closing. Soon they would be back in position to unleash the cannons again. No tricks would save the ship this time. His master's revenge would be visited upon them. None would survive.

Pausing to balance himself, he called out again for more speed.

As the light of the day was starting to fail, the top half of the sails on the front two of the *Buena Vista's* masts suddenly collapsed inward. Rapidly the ship's progress slowed, though it was difficult to discern just how quickly in the stormy conditions.

Thundering forward, the captain on the pursuing ship excitedly saw that they would soon be in firing range. Turning from the bow, he yelled at the gunners to get to their cannons. Returning the spyglass to his eye, he was startled to see the *Buena Vista* much closer than expected and sliding to the right.

Spotting the compressed sails and starboard movement, he suddenly realized what was happening and screamed at the gunners to prepare to fire and for the ship to slow down.

But he had spotted the ruse too late.

Flying through the water, the ship closed the distance too quickly on the deliberately slowing *Buena Vista*. Passing them on the left, their gunners weren't able to get off a shot as the *Buena Vista* unleashed a full cannon round against their starboard side. The cannonballs hit both the cannon deck as well as the rigging that connected the sails to the masts.

As soon as the now-damaged pursuing ship had passed them, the pirates on the mast ladders cut the ropes that had been holding back the sails, and they once again billowed full. Picking up speed, the ship sailed slightly to the side and headed away from the pursuing ship.

The damage inflicted wasn't severe enough to cripple the other ship, but it bought the pirates enough time to lose the vessel during the rainy night that followed.

CHAPTER TWENTY-ONE

TWO HOURS AFTER THE DAWN'S light forced its way through the clouds and illuminated the new day, the *Buena Vista* sailed into the harbor at Elisabethville. The crew had managed to hide the worst of the damage from the cannonballs but knew that they could only disguise that they were a pirate vessel for so long. They had to stop however, as they desperately needed supplies for the wounded. Usually doctors wouldn't provide such things to pirates, but a near universal truth was that enough coins laid on a table erased almost all objections.

Upon acquiring the medicine and supplies, Estevez and the seven men with him returned to the ship and gave it to the ship's doctor. The doctor asked for a few hours to operate on the wounded before they sailed back out.

Heading into town a second time, Estevez deflected the men's inquiries about the person who had attacked them and declared that he needed multiple drinks.

They all headed to a tavern called the Stork's Surprise and settled into two booths near the back. Several bottles of wine were promptly in front of them.

At the same time Estevez and company were settling into the tavern, Captain Umberland, Lightning, Barrel, Parrot and Sam stepped aboard the *Death's Door* and delivered the last of the supplies they had purchased. They had enough muskets, power, shot, swords and knives for the assault on Rojanz. Umberland wished they had more cannons and wasn't totally sure the few they had would be enough, but what they purchased would have to do.

Rounding up the four men, Umberland declared that he wanted a decent meal and some beer before departing on the adventure. The four agreed and followed him back into town, telling the rest of the crew to stay onboard and prepare to depart.

Spotting a pub called the Spitting Walrus, they shared a laugh at the name and headed inside.

Two hours later, Umberland, Lightning, Barrel, Parrot and Sam walked out of the establishment will full bellies and light heads. At the same moment, eight men stumbled out of an establishment across the street called the Stork's Surprise. The two groups shared a laugh at the stumbling walks of the other, but the laughter subsided as the captains got close enough to recognize each other.

"UMBERLAND!" Estevez roared, his cheeks flush from the wine.

"Easy Captain Estevez," Umberland said, backing up. "We're not looking for any trouble."

"UMBERLAND!" Estevez roared again, pulling his sword and lunging toward the man facing him.

The two steps backward that Umberland had taken enabled him enough time to draw his sword and deflect the initial assault. The two groups immediately pulled swords and began battling through the street.

Though they had Umberland's group outnumbered eight-to-five, Estevez's crew was deeper in the grip of the grape and couldn't finish them off.

"Lads follow me!" Umberland shouted and ran down an alley behind them.

Two women were escorting two men across a courtyard when suddenly five pirates sprinted towards them, pursued by eight more. The five turned and attempted to fight the eight while they were still single file in the alley, but they had taken too long to stop and turn around. The battle raged throughout the courtyard before one of the men let go of the lady's hand, stood on a wooden box and yelled, "STOP! STOP!"

After a bit, all the combatants paused and looked at him befuddled.

"These fine ladies and my friend and I are going across this courtyard to that building over there to get familiar. Kindly halt your battle until we've crossed."

Each crew looked at their respective captains who looked at each other, shrugged, and then nodded. All lowered their swords as the two ladies and two men walked past them and into the nearby building.

The second the door shut, Estevez shouted, "Kill them!" and the melee resumed.

Through streets and buildings, the fight raged on. Eventually, Umberland and crew had their backs to the town square as Estevez and his men fought to finish them off. Estevez could see some weariness in his opponent and sensed that the time for his revenge had arrived.

Before he could move in for the kill, 20 British soldiers appeared on the other side of the square and charged at them.

"No! *Mierda!* Back to the ship!" Estevez shouted as the soldiers closed in on Umberland and the other four.

Umberland and his men tried to flee, but since they were closer to the soldiers and hadn't seen them at first, they didn't stand a chance. They were immediately surrounded and fell exhausted to the ground. In any other circumstance they would have fought to the death, knowing what awaited them if they were captured. But after having battled and run for so long against Estevez, they could barely stand. The food and beer in their bellies didn't help either.

All five of them tried to catch their breath as they were disarmed, chained hand and foot, and led away.

Estevez and company rushed down to the dock, jumped aboard the *Buena Vista* and immediately sailed out of the harbor.

Onboard the *Death's Door*, Dogfish had seen people running towards the town square and left the ship to investigate along with Java and Scrag. Following the crowd, they arrived just in time to see Umberland and the others being marched away by the soldiers.

"Now's our chance!" Dogfish exclaimed. "The captain and his loyal scum are all going to swing. We can take the ship!"

The other two nodded enthusiastically and ran behind him as he raced back to the dock. Thundering onto the ship, Dogfish screamed that the captain and the other four had been killed by British soldiers.

"I don't believe it!" said Jenkins.

"It's true!" Java shot back. "We saw it with our own eyes. They're all dead!"

"I saw it too!" Scrag yelled out.

"And they're headed this way Jenkins," Dogfish said, marching up to him. "You either get us out of here now, or we're all dead!"

Jenkins held his ground as several of the other men implored him to listen to reason.

"I don't believe you Dogfish," Jenkins said, the firmness in his eyes cutting through Dogfish's bluster.

"Then get the hell off and be killed too!!" Dogfish screamed. "They're all dead!"

Java started untying the lines that held the ship to the pier, and another of the crew raced to the helm to do the same. Jenkins cursed them all and jumped onto the pier before the ship pulled away. Nine of the crew joined him and they raced towards the town square as the *Death's Door* picked up speed and headed into open water.

Jenkins and the nine men reached the town square and peered into it. People milled around, but there was no sign of any soldiers. Spotting two drunken men conversing and gesturing, Jenkins approached and inquired what was going on. The men informed him that five pirates had been captured alive by the soldiers and marched away. Each man took turns interrupting the other and animatedly reenacting the events described. Thanking them for the information, Jenkins and his group raced across the square in the direction the soldiers had marched the prisoners.

Onboard the *Death's Door*, the remaining crew cheered Dogfish for saving them from certain death at the hands of the British soldiers, unaware of the false nature of the information he'd provided them about the captain. Grandly declaring that he admired the captain and would honor him, he accepted their vote as the ship's new captain. Instead of the traditional crew vote, he insisted that Java be chosen as his first mate. The crew agreed, and Dogfish said that they would head for Rojanz to take the treasure that Umberland had described. First however, he ordered them to sail to Borracho so they could acquire more cannons and he could visit his favorite whorehouse.

CHAPTER TWENTY-TWO

"Defendant Five, Mark Umberland. You are hereby charged with engaging in piracy. How do you plead?"

"Don't give the bastard the satisfaction of an answer Cap'n!" Barrel shouted from the iron cage that the four other defendants were in.

"Silence!" the judge shouted at him, banging his gavel twice for emphasis.

"Sod off you wig-wearing wanker!" Lightning hollered at him.

"We will have order in this court!"

"We will have order in this court!" Parrot said, changing his voice to a far higher key.

"Remove these swine immediately!" the judge screamed, pointing his gavel at them.

Various obscene gestures were hurled the judge's way as the guards shoved them out, clubbing them as they went.

Silence filled the courtroom shortly after their removal.

"Apologies for that Your Honor," Captain Umberland said. "The lads can be a bit feisty sometimes."

"You disgust me more than they do Mr. Umberland."

"So now would be a bad time to tell you to go fuck yourself?"

"Well at least I see where they get it from," the judge said flatly, in that distinctly British upper-class way of expressing disgust without directly stating it.

Captain Umberland smiled broadly at him and nodded affirmatively. He knew the court proceedings were a farce anyway; their fates had been sealed the moment they were captured yesterday. It was all for show, so the British could say they had been fair and delivered an "honorable judgment." The Spanish treated pirates the same way.

Umberland still couldn't believe that they had been captured. It was something he swore he would never allow to happen. Far better to go down with guns blazing than to be chained like dogs and made to sit through this ridiculous proceeding. As he sat pretending to listen to the powdered wigged fool blathering on about how horrible he was, he couldn't help but feel that his last act had finally arrived.

"Oh why don't you just shut the fuck up!?" Captain Umberland suddenly shouted, cutting off the judge mid-sentence.

Horrified at the breach of "the court rules," the judge ordered the guards to remove him.

Moving at double speed, he flew through the charges, heard the evidence and promptly found all five defendants guilty. Death by hanging was the sentence, to be carried out the next day.

A guard stopped by the cell that they were in and casually informed them of the verdict.

None showed any surprise; there was none to show.

"When?" Sam asked.

"Tomorrow before noon."

"What time is it now?"

"About four in the afternoon."

Sam looked over at Captain Umberland, who just shrugged. What could one say?

After the guard left, Barrel turned to the rest and said, "I know it's a long shot, but does anyone have any powder in their pants?"

"I do!" Lightning replied.

"Not now Lightning! Seriously, how can you smile at a time like this?"

"What else is there to do?"

The group glumly agreed, though only Lightning seemed in decent spirits.

After a dinner as miserable in taste as it was melancholy in spirit, the group settled in for the worst night of their lives.

"Hell of a way to go out," Barrel said to Captain Umberland as the two of them leaned against the bars unable to sleep.

"Hell of a way indeed."

The next 12 hours felt like 12 years.

"All right you scum, move it. It's time for the short walk to the long drop, and then to Hell with the lot of you," the guard said the next morning.

It was just past 10 in the morning.

As they were shuffling towards the gallows, Umberland closed his eyes briefly as the wind blew over his face. The smell of the sea accompanied it, and he felt a great sadness that this was the last time he would experience that wonderful smell. He knew he would never feel the cooling wind upon his face again. Spying the horrible contraption in the distance, he shook his head. After all their adventures, after all that they had been through, for it to end like this… wearing Old Roger's necktie.

To his left, he spotted four guards escorting nine prisoners in the opposite direction. "Off to the courthouse today, then following us to the gallows tomorrow," he muttered to himself. "See you fellas in Hell."

Somehow the thought made him smile. Above him, the birds were flying, the sun was shining and the wind was blowing.

As the four guards and nine prisoners passed them, the prisoners suddenly threw their arms out and the shackles fell free. The four "guards" broke into two groups and ran up to the two guards ahead and behind

Umberland's group. They immediately fired their muskets, killing all four. The nine prisoners who had shaken off the fake shackles ran to the gallows with pistols out and finished off the three solders. Then they forced the hangman's hooded head into the noose, spat on it and pulled the lever, releasing the trapdoor beneath him.

The four men who had disguised themselves as guards grabbed the keys from the dead soldiers, freed Umberland and the other four, joined up with the nine fake prisoners, and they all headed towards the far wall.

"Who the hell are these guys!?" Sam shouted to Umberland.

"Who cares? They're saving our ass!" Barrel yelled.

"We'll never get over it!" Parrot said as they approached the outer barrier.

As they reached the wall, two figures appeared on top of it holding a ladder. They lowered it to the men below and helped them up one at a time.

"Quickly!" Captain Umberland shouted, seeing the British soldiers pouring into the square behind them.

The last of the group scrambled up and then hurried down the ladder that was placed on the other side. As they were racing down the hill away from the fort, the first three British soldiers appeared on the wall behind them. Suddenly shots rang out from the bushes to the left and the three soldiers fell off the wall dead. Two more soldiers popped their heads above the wall and were promptly dropped as well.

"Who is shooting!?" one of the rescuers shouted.

Out of the bushes near the fort's outer wall, 10 men emerged and started running after them.

"Jenkins!" Umberland shouted, spotting the man at the head of the group.

"We're here Captain!" came the response, along with several others with similar declarations.

The rescuers raced through the town's backstreets. Leaving the town behind, they ran over two small hills and down a third that led to the water's edge.

"Holy shit!" Lightning said upon seeing the large pirate ship anchored just off shore. Three small boats were tied to the rocks. The 18 men, joined by Jenkins and the other nine, boarded the boats and rowers immediately started pulling at their oars, straining against the unexpected weight of the 10 additional men.

"Jenkins! Great to see you!" Lightning said, throwing his arms around him.

"You too buddy! Wish it was under better circumstances, but I'm glad you're all alive!"

"Jenkins, where's the *Death's Door*?!" Umberland shouted from one of the other boats.

"Tell you later Captain," was his muted response.

Umberland and the four with him looked across at the long faces of the 10 men on the other boats. Umberland nodded solemnly and turned his attention towards the large ship they were heading for. The other four with him shook their heads silently. No one talked until they reached the ship.

As soon as they arrived, everyone was hauled aboard. The three small boats were left bobbing in the water. On land, the British soldiers were coming into view at the top of the hill. The ship was out of musket range and they had no cannons with them, but all the pirates knew a warship full of soldiers would soon be departing the island in pursuit.

With sails out full, the pirate ship picked up speed and surged away from the island.

Standing on top of the hill, the fort's senior officer, Commander Quint, gripped his spyglass and followed the departing ship. His face burned with rage.

Onboard, a large figure made his way down the stairs below deck. Reaching the hold where the five freed men were being kept along with the 10 who had unexpectedly helped in the rescue, the man stood in the doorway. His frame took up the entire space.

Looking up, Umberland did a double take and said, "Captain Estevez!? *You* saved us?"

"That's right you dog. I should have let you swing Umberland, but that wouldn't be right. To hell with the English. *They* don't get to kill you. Only *I* get to kill you!"

Silence filled the room as the men stared at Estevez.

"So you saved us, just to kill us?" Lightning said.

"Silence!" boomed Estevez.

"If you're going to" Lightning started to say, but stopped when Umberland grabbed his arm.

"What are your intentions Captain?" Umberland said to Estevez.

"My intentions? To kill you of course. But not today. Not like this. We're taking you to Borracho. The British are going to be looking for this ship; for all of us. They'll want their revenge too. Borracho will provide us with a safe haven and will enable you to get back on your feet. You're a respected captain, though I don't know why you scoundrel! But for whatever reason, you are liked. Someone on the island will help you get a ship, and you can rebuild your crew from there. Looks like you still have a core of solid men here with you. Then, once you've gotten a new ship and raised a new crew, I can find you out there somewhere and kill you honorably."

"Sounds fair to me. We're indebted to you Captain. You saved us all."

"Don't remind me."

"Before we never speak of this again, may I inquire how you did it?"

Estevez gestured for the men to follow him. He headed back up to the deck.

Most of the crew were on deck. Bottles of whiskey and wine were being passed around. After a nod from Estevez, they were passed to Umberland and his men too. As the bottles continued to make the rounds and fresh ones were opened, Estevez pointed to Javier and said, "Tell them the tale."

Javier took a long pull from a bottle of burgundy and said, "Months ago, we attacked a Spanish town and acquired their treasure. We were disappointed in the lack of gold, but suddenly Plato noticed the red uniforms folded in a corner. Apparently they had captured some English soldiers and taken their uniforms. The uniforms were stored in the town and we immediately recognized the value in obtaining them. We've been waiting for the right moment to use them; lucky you."

"Indeed," said Umberland.

Estevez drank from a bottle and said, "After you were captured and we had escaped, I sent five of my men back to the island and they looked over the fort you were being held in. We bribed a local boy to go ask one of the soldiers on guard when the captured men would be executed, and he informed us of the time."

Umberland nodded and raised his wine bottle in appreciation. Taking a pull, he looked at Jenkins and inquired what happened to the *Death's Door*.

Jenkins related the tale of Dogfish telling the crew that Umberland and the other four had been killed, and then taking off in the ship.

The men onboard the *Buena Vista* shook their heads. A few laughed and told Umberland he had no kind of luck.

"The crew believed Dogfish?" Barrel said.

"Most did. Those two little shits, Scrag and Java, backed him up saying that you were dead."

"A mutiny," said Umberland.

"Essentially. The nine who are with me are the only ones who refused to believe him. They risked their lives to help save you guys too."

"Eternal gratitude lads," Umberland said, walking around and bear hugging each of them.

Pausing in front of Jenkins, he shook his hand and said, "Most appreciated my friend. More than I can relate in words."

"It was my honor Captain."

Both men nodded at one another.

Estevez walked over and instructed all of them to remain in the hold, far out of sight, until they reached Borracho.

Part 7:
Pirate's Life

PAGE INTENTIONALLY LEFT BLANK

CHAPTER TWENTY-THREE

THE VELVET CLAM was one of the more respectable whorehouses in Ciudad Borracho. The three-story house of ill repute was well furnished and advertised itself as the finest establishment in the Caribbean. The owner was in her early 50s and called herself Busty More, though her real name was Sarah McMillan. She was a walking cliché; Scotch-Irish with a fiery temper who could drink most men under the table. However she was fair to the ladies who worked there and ran the place professionally. She was always available to help with whatever they needed and was violently protective of them, something many a disrespectful man had found out the hard way. She knew all the pub owners in the blocks that surrounded her establishment and there wasn't a one who wouldn't come immediately to her aid if she ever called for help. Though rarely did a situation arise that she couldn't handle herself. She had personally killed five men who either were out of control, or had threatened to harm one of the ladies.

On this particular night, she was in the first floor bar area enjoying a whiskey and chatting with one of the two men who served as bartenders. On the second floor, two of the ladies were entertaining two very drunk pirates; Scrag and Java. Both had finished in under a minute and the ladies were merely killing time before showing them the door. It had been a slow night so far, though it was still only an hour past midnight.

"You know...you girls are lucky! You're in the presence of master pirates," Java boasted, barely managing to keep hold of his bottle of rum.

"Really?" one of the ladies responded, completely disinterested.

"That's right!" Scrag said, clumsily throwing his arm around his friend's shoulder. "Our captain got captured, but fuck him. We didn't save him. We took his ship instead!"

Both of them broke out into high-pitched laughter. Too much alcohol always made their laughs horribly offensive.

The ladies could barely contain their disgust. One of them asked who the captain was and Scrag responded that his name was Umberland, but he was dead now. The British hung him and the other four for sure, he declared emphatically.

"Anyway, we sail under Captain Dogfish now! We rule the seas! Master pirates feared by all!" Java slurred out, slashing the air for emphasis.

Leaning closer and disgusting the ladies even more with the harshness of his booze-filled breath, Scrag whispered to them, "We're setting off on a mighty quest. We're going to sack a Spanish town that's full of gold."

"Sure you are."

"It's true," said Java. He too leaned in and lowered his voice unnecessarily. "The dead captain told us about it. But he is dead now, so fuck him. The gold is ours!"

"Shush!" Scrag slurred.

"You shush!"

"Don't mind my friend here; he's drunk. But he speaks the truth. The Spanish town doesn't know that the greatest pirates in the world are coming for their treasure."

The ladies nodded their heads and wished them good luck. Rising to their feet, they led the two to the door. They bade them goodnight as the two attempted to blow kisses their way and stumbled into the street declaring they would buy Borracho when they returned.

"What a pair of assholes," one of the ladies said.

The other simply nodded and they went off to find Busty.

"Welcome back. How were they?" Busty asked upon seeing them enter.

Shaking their heads and letting the expressions on their face say more than words, the two grabbed a glass of wine each and sat down at her table.

"That bad eh?"

"Worse."

"Tell her about them stealing their captain's ship and leaving him to get captured and hung by the British."

"What!?"

"That's right. That's one of the many things they related, along with how great they were in bed and how lucky we were to have had the honor of bedding them."

"Yeah, all 48 seconds of their half-masted grunting."

"Seriously. Anyway, apparently they saw their captain getting captured and didn't do anything to save him. They just let him and four of their fellow pirates get taken. Then they went back to the ship, declared that they saw him die, and took off."

"Animals! No loyalty! Nothing I hate more than cowardly men; especially cowardly pirates!"

"Now they're planning to sail to some Spanish town and steal their gold, which is simply a plan they stole from their dead captain."

"Disrespecting him even in death! Did they say what town they were planning to attack?"

"No."

"Any details about it? What region it was in? Anything?"

"Nope, the only name they said was of their former captain; Umberland. They just said that it was his plan and they were going to carry it out. They said the town had more gold than any other town in the New World and they were going to be so rich upon their return that they would buy Borracho."

"Bullshit! Boasting, lying and exaggerating about everything; just like a man. Any idea when they are planning to depart?"

"Tomorrow is what they said."

Finishing her whiskey in one gulp, she called out to the man behind the bar, "Horst! Watch the place for a few!"

Getting up, she stuck two pistols in slots she had added to her dress, picked up the serrated knife she always had nearby and headed out the door.

Walking through the streets looking for the two men, Busty was unable to find them. She started asking random people if they had seen two very drunk men recently. Ignoring the multiple wisecracks that were said in return, she finally found a man who informed her that two men had crashed into him and knocked the food out of his hand. He directed her to the street that they had headed down, and she set off in pursuit.

Reaching the water, she spotted the two men barely able to stand, dragging themselves towards a large ship that had *Death's Door* painted on the stern. The men fell over backward onto the pier and had to be hauled aboard by some of the other pirates.

"Scum," she said to herself and walked back into town. She headed to multiple pubs, told the owners about what she had learned, and asked them to see if anyone knew of a pirate ship called the *Death's Door*. She also related the passing of Captain Umberland.

As she was leaving one of the pubs, a man followed her out and approached her.

"Pardon me *Madame*, but I was in the bar just now and couldn't help overhearing part of your conversation. Did you say that Captain Umberland has been killed?"

"Presumably. He was captured by British soldiers."

"Undoubtedly on his way to the gallows. Do you know when this happened?"

"Sounds like a couple of days ago; maybe three or four?"

"He is gone for sure then. Very sad news."

"You knew him?"

"Only by reputation. He was known as one of the best pirate captains around. Damn fine fellow. Never got the chance to meet him unfortunately."

"And you are?"

"Oh, my apologies *Madame*! My name is Captain Jacques le Pinard Montpellier. And you are?"

"My name is Busty More. Pleasure to meet you Captain. I have heard of you."

"Oh? Good things no doubt!"

"Good enough. You should stop by my establishment sometime."

"And what establishment might that be *Madame?*"

"The Velvet Clam. Best whorehouse in the Caribbean."

"Many have made the same boast."

"Many aren't us."

"Indeed. I like your verve! I believe I have heard of this establishment. I will absolutely pay you a visit before I depart."

"I look forward to it Captain. Bring friends."

Captain Montpellier bowed, and they parted ways.

In another part of town, Jenny and Alice were drinking heavily at a tavern called the Weather Gage. Earlier in the day they'd had a small tiff, but it had blown over quickly and they were back on good terms by the time night arrived.

Neither had eaten much for dinner and at the start of the night, they'd had the bad luck of running into four pirates just in from a successful raid. The four threw money and drinks at them, and all six made the old mistake of drinking too much too quickly.

The two ladies easily deflected the men's clumsy attempts at moving things forward and departed, throwing thank-you's over their shoulder as they left.

After visiting another pub, they ended up at the Weather Gage and were deep in the drink's grip as the hour passed midnight.

Jenny was talking to two well-dressed pirates who sailed under the command of the feared Captain Blueblood. Captain Blueblood came from an extremely rich Italian noble family, but the family had disowned him when he chose to pursue a life of piracy. Unlike most other pirates, Blueblood chose to become a pirate because it allowed him to hunt humans for sport. The family was a patron of the arts and very respected in Bologna. The actions of their wayward son broke their hearts and they vowed never to utter his name again after word of his atrocities reached them.

The two men were Alesemo and Andolini. Alesemo was Captain Blueblood's first mate. Both possessed the deadly combination of charm and confidence that some psychopaths somehow are born with. Those two traits, combined with the natural attraction women often have to dangerous men, made them irresistible to young Alice. The overload of alcohol didn't help.

Jenny had been under the weather for a few days, but continued raging just as hard as ever. As Alice talked to Alesemo and Andolini, she was at a nearby table drinking with O'Malley, the first mate of the pirate ship *Green Thunder*. The ship was commanded by Captain Sean Stoutheart. He had chosen the name due to his love of stout, the strong dark beer brewed to perfection in his hometown of Cork, in the southern part of Ireland.

Earlier in the night, O'Malley had insisted he could drink Jenny under the table. Two hours later, he was fighting to stay on his stool. Jenny was in a similar predicament, but hiding it better.

When Alice was in the company of a man she liked, she had the horrible habit of making snide comments at Jenny's expense to try and impress him. This was one of the worst aspects of her personality, and one that drove Jenny absolutely up the wall. After talking with Alesemo and Andolini for a bit, Alice had begun to fall into her old habit. Jenny, further into the drink than she should have been and suffering from her cold, was in no mood for that shit and soon left the table to talk with O'Malley. Soon after joining him, he had mentioned being able to drink her under the table and she, angry at Alice, quickly accepted the challenge.

Now as the hour marched towards one in the morning, O'Malley finished another tankard of beer and watched bleary-eyed as Jenny coughed, lowered her tankard for a second, and then shakily raised it again to finish it off.

When she set it down on the table empty, he smiled at her and slurred out, "You're fading lassie. Why don't you call it?"

He smiled at her for two more seconds, then fell sideways off his stool onto the ground and began snoring loudly.

Jenny laughed at him and declared herself the winner. She looked over at Alice triumphantly, but Alice just rolled her eyes and whispered something to the two men that caused both to start laughing while looking in Jenny's direction.

Moving away from her stool towards the bar, Jenny found walking difficult and realized that she was drunker than she had imagined while sitting down; a predicament familiar to all drinkers.

Steadying herself, she went back to Alice's table and announced that she was ready to call it a night. Alice looked up indifferently and declared that she was having fun and was staying. Jenny pushed for her to leave, but Alice looked back at the two men and dismissively waved her hand at Jenny.

Angry, drunk and sick, Jenny shook her head and told Alice she was a big girl and could do whatever she wanted. With that, Jenny made her way out of the tavern and painfully walked back to their room at a nearby inn.

The sun was at its zenith when Jenny awoke the next day and squinted against its brightness. She had thrown up before going to bed the night before, something she almost never did. Alice wasn't in the bed with her. Jenny looked around the room, but it was in a state of disarray, as was their habit.

Throwing some clothes on, she looked for Alice downstairs but couldn't find her. The Innkeeper didn't seem to recall seeing her that morning, though he couldn't be sure.

Making her way back to the Weather Gage, Jenny banged on the door until the proprietor gingerly opened it and told her they were closed. Grabbing the door before he could finish closing it, she described her friend and the events of the night before. The part about the snoring Irishman jogged his memory and he said her friend had loudly left with two Italian pirates. Jenny pressed him to remember anything more, and he finally told her that he thought they said something about how beautiful the moonlight was bouncing off the water of the lake in the middle of the island. Alice was excited about this and declared she wanted to see it, and they all left together.

Thanking him for the information, Jenny found new life in her legs and rushed towards the nearest path that led through the hills to the lake. Gasping for breath as she crossed the final hill, she looked down at the lake's rich, blue waters. Calling out Alice's name repeatedly, she headed down to the water's edge and began moving circularly around it.

A short while later, a loud groan and muffled cry from behind her caused her to whirl and head into the bushes. Spotting two legs sticking out from some tall grass, she screamed Alice's name and rushed over to the figure.

The sight of Alice's bloodied and badly beaten face caused her to gasp and cover her mouth for a second. Gathering the groaning Alice in her arms, she apologized profusely for leaving her alone the night before and promised her that she would be fine.

Alice fought through her bloody mouth to apologize for her behavior the night before, but Jenny quickly shushed her and said everything was all right. Imploring her to save her strength, Jenny worked to make her as comfortable as possible while continuing to whisper about all the adventures they would have once she recovered.

The words made Alice smile weakly, and she painfully reached up to stroke Jenny's face. Tears welled in Jenny's eyes as Alice fought through repeated coughs to tell her how much she loved her and that she treasured every minute they had spent together, especially the past few weeks.

Jenny echoed the statements and continued to tell her that she would be all right, as Alice tried to smile.

After making Alice as comfortable as possible, Jenny rushed back to town in search of help. As luck would have it, in the first place she entered she ran into Billy and Bob Boots, the two men who had assisted her and Alice during the fight at the Powder & Shot tavern. The three of them broke off a tabletop and headed back to where Alice lay.

Using the tabletop as a makeshift stretcher, Billy and Bob carried her back to town, while Jenny continued to whisper words of comfort. They moved her into the room she shared with Jenny and gently placed her in bed. One of them ran to get a doctor.

"Is she going to be all right?" Jenny said, gripping the doctor's arm as he exited the room.

"She got pretty roughed up, but she's strong and should pull through," he replied, shutting the door to the room behind him. "She needs plenty of rest. No exertion, no booze, no excitement. Understood?"

"Completely."

"Good. I'll check back in on her tomorrow to see how she's doing."

Turning to Billy and Bob, Jenny expressed her gratitude for their assistance. They shared their disgust with what the two men had done to Alice and vowed to help Jenny take her revenge on them if she so needed it.

"We sail under Captain Burnley aboard the ship *Wharf Rat*," Billy said. "We're supposed to be heading out soon, but we'll check in on you before we depart."

While Jenny stayed and watched over Alice, Bob offered to head back to the pub they were at the night before to find out who the two men were. Jenny would have normally declined such an offer and done it herself, but she couldn't leave Alice alone right now, and she didn't want too much time to pass before confronting the owner about the men. She thanked them both again and said it was very kind of them to offer, and she would be grateful for any information they could obtain.

Both men left and immediately headed to the Weather Gage. The proprietor wanted nothing to do with them and attempted to slam the door in their faces. Two punches to the gut and a knife against his nuts quickly changed things, and he rapidly queried his staff about the two men.

Armed with a description of the two, as well as their names, Billy and Bob went from bar to bar until they found someone who knew which ship they were on. They belonged to the crew of the *Bellissimo*, commanded by Captain Blueblood. Heading to the docks, they discovered that the ship had departed earlier that day.

A few days passed, and Alice improved enough to stand and walk a bit. Jenny knew of a good doctor back in New Seville and she decided that they would head there so Alice could fully recover. Jenny had the information about the two men who had committed the assault, but revenge would have to wait.

Billy and Bob Boots checked in on them and when they heard that the women were heading to New Seville, they spoke to a pirate captain that they knew who was familiar with the location.

The man's real name was Stewart MacGregor, but everyone knew him as Captain Walrus due to his bushy mustache, and his propensity to roar with either laughter or anger. He commanded the vessel *Drunken Pipers* and said he was the most wanted man in his native Scotland. He was heading to New Seville in three days and when he heard what had happened to Alice, and that she and Jenny were friends with the owner of the Crazy Goat pub, he personally assured their safety onboard his ship.

Billy and Bob informed Jenny that they had to get back to the *Wharf Rat* because they were leaving tomorrow. They promised to visit her the next time they were in New Seville, and the three of them hugged goodbye.

After they left, Alice looked up at Jenny and said, "I don't want the adventure to end. I don't care that this happened. We're two badass women and I don't want one stupid night to ruin everything. I don't want to go back to that little island and lead a little life."

"Oh my sweet one, nothing is ending. We just need to get you all healed up. Then the adventure will most certainly continue! Once you are better, we are going to hunt down the two bastards who did this to you and exact a most horrific revenge upon them!"

"Yeah! We'll show them just who they fucked with!"

"Exactly! You rest up now. Soon we depart for New Seville. We'll regroup there, find out what we can about the two pirates that did this, and then head off again! To grab life by the horns and make it ours!"

CHAPTER TWENTY-FOUR

"UMBERLAND! WE'RE HERE," Captain Estevez yelled down into the hold as the *Buena Vista* floated into Ciudad Borracho's harbor. Ropes were tossed over and the ship was secured to the pier.

"Much obliged Captain, for everything."

"Just get off."

Captain Umberland and the 14 men with him walked past the glaring members of the crew and stepped off the ship.

"Umberland. You'll need this," Estevez said, following them off the ship.

He pushed a small cloth bag with some coins into his hand.

"It's not much, but it's enough for you and your men to live on for about a week, unless you drink it away."

"Thank you again Captain."

"Stop thanking me Umberland. People know you here; someone will loan you enough to purchase some sort of a vessel. In the meantime, use the coins wisely, but never forget that I'm out there looking for you. This doesn't erase what you did. Now get out of my sight before my better judgment kicks in."

Umberland nodded and led his men down the pier into town. Estevez waited until they were out of sight and told Sausalito to come with him into town. He gave extra coins to those who had participated in the rescue and told the crew to go have a good time.

The night passed as scandalously as ever on the island, and dawn's light brought the pain of morning to all.

That afternoon, four men were walking down one of the roads when they overheard two people discussing some news. One of the four introduced himself as Captain Van Muis and asked them to repeat what they had just said. Upon hearing it, he broke into a run towards the nearest bar and vigorously threw open the door, the other three arriving a few seconds later.

The Broken Anchor was a medium-sized, one-story room. The interior was one of the darkest on the island. Each time the door opened, the brightness from outside illuminated the room and its inhabitants. Then when it shut, pitch darkness returned. After about 10 seconds or so, the eyes of those who just entered would adjust enough to find an empty booth along the walls, or a chair at the bar that faced the door. After a couple of minutes, they were able to mostly see around the room. Known for their tequila and food (the chili con carne enchiladas were especially popular), the establishment also featured a selection of quality rum.

"HE'S DEAD!" Captain Van Muis shouted upon entering. "DEAD!" he repeated, squinting against the darkness. "Dead I say! DEAD! YES!" he continued, throwing his arms out wide and dancing around in almost a full circle with his head thrown back. He broke into loud laughter. "Oh thank God. It's so beautiful. Just when you think there are no more miracles left in this world," he said, dropping into seat with a giant smile on his face.

"Who is dead Sir?" the man behind the bar asked him.

"That dirty, filthy, no good son-of-a-bitch! That's who!"

"Oh, I see... him."

Van Muis threw the bartender a hard look, but then immediately the smile returned to his face. "It doesn't matter what you say; you can't make me upset on a day that has brought such beautiful news." With that he stood up, walked over to the bar, leaned across it and with the giant smile still on his face, looked the bartender right in the eyes and said, "He's dead."

Breaking into a laugh again, he gestured at the three men who had come in behind him and said, "A bottle of your finest rum for me and my men; for today we celebrate!" Returning to the table with a flourish, he threw his arms out wide and shouted to the entire room, "HE'S DEAD!!"

Arriving at the table with a bottle of rum, the bartender spread out the four beakers and filled them. Settling the bottle on the table, he turned to leave. Van Muis grabbed his arm, pushed the bottle against his chest and said, "I insist you have a drink with us. I am Captain Van Muis, the greatest of the Dutch pirates! Today we celebrate the death of the dirtiest pig on this godforsaken island! Lift 'em up fellas! We drink to the death of Captain Umberland!"

The four men downed their beakers while the bartender took a short pull from the bottle. He quickly set it on the table and headed back behind the bar.

"What's your problem little rabbit? Are you a rabbit?" Van Muis said, staring at the bartender. "Look at the way he scampered back there like a little girl hiding in her room," he said to his men as they burst out laughing.

The other three joined in the mockery, yelling increasingly idiotic comparisons and punctuating each one with shots of rum. The bartender proceeded to clean glasses next to the multiple pistols and knives hidden behind the bar. He had heard it all during his time on the island and the group's increasingly drunken shouts bounced off his iron hide. But he was keeping a much closer eye on them than they suspected.

"I kicked Umberland's ass one night at a bar called the Crazy Goat in New Seville!" Van Muis said after taking a pull straight from the bottle. "Dutchmen can't be beat! We kick the crap out of any English dogs that dare cross our path!"

"I'm surprised you're not fighting for your country right now Sir, seeing as how you're such a patriot," the bartender said while looking down at the glass he was cleaning with a towel. "No desire to return home and assist in fighting the English? The Second Anglo-Dutch War broke out last year, as I'm sure you're aware."

"Fuck the Dutch Republic!" Van Muis shouted. "I love my people, but the government can kiss my orange ass! I sail for myself alone! I owe allegiance to no nation, only to myself!"

"To the captain!" one of his men shouted, and they all downed their beakers.

"To the death of Umberland!" Van Muis shouted, and they all slammed fresh shots.

"Another bottle!" the man closest to the bar shouted to the bartender.

"And we're not paying for it!" Van Muis hollered. "That's what you get for your cute little comment about the Second Anglo-Dutch War. Bring us another bottle immediately little rabbit! Then hop your bunny ass back behind the bar!"

All four burst out laughing as the bartender walked over a fresh bottle.

A couple of the regulars looked at the bartender as he walked back to the bar and moved their eyes quickly between him and the table of four, then back again. He smiled and shook his head slightly.

Tossing the empty rum bottle into a barrel, the bartender watched as a man rose from one of the booths in the back and walked rapidly up to the table of four.

"VAN MUIS!" the man shouted, causing virtually the entire bar to jump.

Whirling to his feet, Van Muis stared wide-eyed at the man in front of him and let out the highest-pitched squeak anyone had ever heard inside that particular pub.

With one compact punch, the man knocked him to the floor. He was unconscious before he hit it.

Staring at the other three who had risen to their feet and were looking at him equally shocked, the man let out a primal scream that chilled the other pirates in the room. The three men utter variations on the high-pitched squeak of their floored captain, then turned and ran out of the establishment in a cartoonish fashion.

As two of the regulars dragged the unconscious Van Muis out of the place, after relieving him of his money of course, the bartender looked at the man standing in the middle of the room with his fists still clenched and said, "And who might you be good Sir?"

"Call me Umberland."

The bartender's eyes went as wide as everyone else's before being replaced with an even larger smile. "Umberland? As in Captain Umberland I assume?"

"Correct."

"Apparently the news of your demise is quite premature."

"Apparently."

"Scary punch you have Captain."

"Thank you."

"I think your scream is even scarier."

"Indeed."

"If you would care to return to your two companions over in the booth, I would be happy to provide you all with some rum on the house. That was awesome!"

"Much obliged."

With that, Umberland returned to his booth as the bartender produced a bottle of rum and three beakers.

PAGE INTENTIONALLY LEFT BLANK

CHAPTER TWENTY-FIVE

CAPTAIN MONTPELLIER APPROACHED the Broken Anchor with his heart heavy from a piece of news he had recently heard. Suddenly the door burst open and three men ran past him screaming. A few moments later, a fourth man was carried out unconscious and dumped on the ground. The three who had run down the road finally stopped and were gingerly approaching the unconscious figure as Montpellier moved past him and entered the establishment.

He took a few seconds to adjust his eyes, then headed to the bar and ordered a rum. Raising the beaker up, he cast his eyes to the ceiling and then downed the drink in one go.

"Solemn vows Sir?" the bartender asked him from behind the bar.

"Drinking to the memory of a fine pirate, taken from us too soon."

"As they all are. May I ask his name?"

"Captain Umberland. Never did learn his first name. Only ever heard him called Captain Umberland, or simply Umberland."

The proprietor let out a laugh.

"You think it's funny!?" Captain Montpellier snapped, pulling out a dagger as he spoke.

"Easy fella! Easy! I didn't mean no disrespect."

"No disrespect!? You laugh at the memory of a fallen pirate captain and then compound the insult by calling me 'fella' instead of captain?"

"I wasn't aware you were a captain. My deepest apologies, truly."

Captain Montpellier sheathed his dagger and nodded his acceptance of the apology.

The man set a fresh rum in front of him and said, "This one's on me Captain."

Montpellier thanked the man and insisted he have one with him. The man obliged. When they had finished, the bartender said, "The only reason I laughed earlier is that you have been greatly misinformed."

"What do you mean?"

The bartender pointed towards a booth in one of the corners with three men at it and said, "The fella on the left over there? *That's* Captain Umberland."

"What!?" Montpellier exclaimed, jerking his head towards the booth, squinting against the darkness. "Are you sure?"

"100 percent."

Walking slowly across the room with his head leaning forward as if unsure what he was seeing, Montpellier approached the booth.

The three men sitting at it looked up at him cautiously.

"I'm sorry to interrupt you gentlemen, but you wouldn't happen to be Captain Umberland would you?"

The man on the left side of the booth responded in the affirmative and stood up.

"Captain Umberland! You're alive!" Montpellier shouted, throwing his arms around him.

Startled, Umberland stood still as Montpellier gave him a large hug.

Letting go, Montpellier straightened his jacket and said, "My apologies for the informality Captain, but it's a great relief to see you. The word around town is that you had been captured by the British and hung."

"We were captured by the British, but were rescued literally as we were being marched to the gallows."

"What luck!"

"Sorry friend, but I'm unfamiliar with your face. Who are you?"

"How rude of me! I am Captain Jacques le Pinard Montpellier."

"Montpellier...Captain Montpellier! Of the ship *Cheval*? I'm an admirer of your exploits!"

"As I am of yours good Sir."

"Captain Montpellier, let me introduce you to two of my finest friends and crew members. On the left is Barrel, my first mate. On the right is Jenkins, helmsman and leader of the 10 crew members who didn't join the mutiny."

"Mutiny! What mutiny?"

"First we need more drinks. Please join us Captain, I insist."

"The drinks are on me. I insist!"

"Most generous of you. Jenkins, grab us four more rums."

"Aye Captain."

Upon his return with the drinks, Captain Umberland relayed the tale of running into Captain Estevez and getting captured by the British soldiers at the end of the fight. Then Jenkins relayed Dogfish's betrayal and his part in the rescue.

"So let me get this straight, Captain Estevez wants you dead, but he saved you so he could do it personally?" Montpellier said when they were finished.

"That's correct," Umberland responded.

"Estevez is young and hasn't been pirating for as long as we have, but he normally has good character and sound judgment. Do you know why he wants you dead?"

Barrel and Jenkins started to laugh a bit, though they struggled to contain it as Umberland cast a look at them.

"Well..." Umberland said. "You see, I may have... I mean, I sort of..."

"He plowed his wife," Jenkins interjected.

"I beg your pardon?"

"I slept with Captain Estevez's wife," Umberland said, taking a drink of rum.

Barrel and Jenkins tried hard, but couldn't keep from breaking into a proper laugh. Montpellier soon joined in.

"Oh I see," Montpellier said, regaining his composure. "Well that would certainly explain his animosity towards you."

"I didn't know it was his wife at the time," Umberland said flatly.

"Did you find out later?"

"It may have been brought to my attention shortly after the fact. If I had known who she was, I never would have slept with her."

"Indeed. Bad luck I suppose."

Finishing their drinks, Montpellier asked Barrel and Jenkins to give him a moment alone with Umberland. The two men nodded and headed to the bar. Umberland insisted on buying him another rum, which the proprietor promptly brought over.

"To Captain Umberland," Montpellier said, raising his beaker. "Plunderer of the Spanish treasure ship *Golena*, the man who led the crew in taking four ships in one day, the wild man from Cumberland!"

"To Captain Montpellier," Umberland replied, also raising his beaker. "The Bane of the Spanish Main, conqueror of Santa Dominaco, and third generation scallywag!"

"Fourth generation actually; *Störtebeker!*"

"*Störtebeker!*"

Both men downed their drinks and nodded at each other.

Captain Montpellier shared the tale of his recent sacking of Saint Fermin and mentioned that soon he was setting off on his grandest adventure yet, though he would share no further details.

As the conversation fell silent, Montpellier shifted in his chair and said, "Tell me Captain… not to bring up an awkward subject, but how much money do you have?"

Umberland let out a humorless laugh, reached into his coat and dropped a small bag onto the table.

"That's it?"

"That's it. Captain Estevez left the 14 of us enough money to last about six days. This is what we've got left."

"Wait here. I'll be back in 15 minutes."

Strolling back into the establishment a short time later, Montpellier returned to the booth and sat across from Umberland. Reaching into his coat, he removed two bags of coins and set them on the table. "Here Captain," he said. "Take these and use the money to get back on your feet."

"That is very generous of you, but I cannot accept. It's too much."

"I insist. What Dogfish did was shameful. Disgraceful. No way for a pirate to act against a captain such as yourself. The two men of yours at the bar, and the others who stayed loyal after you were captured, are a testament to your character. We need more decent scallywags like all of you. Use this money to acquire a new ship and raise supplies. Then go hunt down that swine Dogfish and take your vengeance! One day in the future, I'm sure you'll find a way to repay me."

"I'm humbled by your graciousness Captain. I swear, I'll pay you back and then some."

"I know. I wish I could tell you where Dogfish was headed, but all I heard was that he was going to attack a Spanish town. Sadly that could be anywhere. I don't know which one."

"I do."

Montpellier looked at him surprised, and then broke into a wide smile and nodded admirably. "Good luck then *Monsieur*! Happy hunting!"

"Thank you Captain Montpellier, for everything! May wine, women and fortune fill your future!"

PAGE INTENTIONALLY LEFT BLANK

CHAPTER TWENTY-SIX

FIVE DAYS LATER, Captain Estevez and Sausalito entered a tavern on the other side of town called the Red Cape.

The bar was oval and stood in the center of the circular room. Three circular stairwells led up the balcony that wrapped around the entire room. Tables and chairs were spread throughout it, as well as individual rooms used by the ladies who worked for the establishment. Very thin slides leading from the balcony down to the main room were used to pour shots from upstairs to patrons below. Four chandeliers hung from the ceiling, and torches were added to the pillars supporting the balcony.

A stage big enough for three people was upstairs, facing the door. Tonight, the great pirate guitarist Cap'n Joe was playing alone. He was widely considered the best guitarist on the island. He was furiously strumming the guitar, as the music reverberating around the room. Estevez and Sausalito ordered their second bottle of wine and sat down at a table in front of the balcony overhang.

"Hey handsome, heads-up!" one of the ladies hollered down to them.

Sausalito looked at the woman who was about to pour a shot down one of the slides and broke into a wide grin.

"Not you!" she yelled at him.

"Sorry *amigo*," Estevez said laughing. Looking up at the woman, he winked at her and drank the shot that she poured down the slide. He winked at her again and then looked back at Sausalito and said, "Her rack was better than yours."

"Fuck you... Captain."

"Fuck you... First Mate!"

Estevez kept grinning at Sausalito and then said, "Drink!" as he goofy poured each of them more wine, half spilling each cup.

"Nice pour," Sausalito replied laughing.

"Oh, *now* you want to laugh!?"

"*Now* something funny happened!"

"Ahhhh, you're hopeless!" Estevez said, picking up his wine and downing it, spilling half of what remaining in the cup onto his jacket. "*Mierda*."

Sausalito grinned at him until he finally shook his head and said, "Okay, maybe it's a little funny."

"OH MY GOD! GET DOWN FROM THERE!" a lady screamed at a man who had somehow managed to jump from the upper balcony onto one of the large chandeliers.

Everyone below looked up at the man as he used his weight to start swinging it back and forth.

"Sherman! Get down from there you crazy bastard!" one of the pirates yelled at him as he began to get some good distance between swings. "I don't care how important your inventions are to our protection, get the hell off the chandelier!"

Shouting incoherently as loud as he could, the man began to "stab" the air with an imaginary sword as he swung. After a minute of this, he let out a scream as he lost his grip and fell, smashing through a table. The room went silent as everyone stared at the crumbled figure surrounded by what remained of the table.

"Bahhahahahahaha! I AM INVINCIBLE!" the man on the floor shouted, throwing off pieces of wood and suddenly thundering to his feet, stunning everyone in the pub.

"Sherman! You lunatic! Come over here and have a drink with us," Captain Estevez called out to the man. "It would be an honor to buy a round for the man whose genius helps keep scallywag strongholds safe throughout the Caribbean."

The man dusted himself off, rapidly made his way over to their table and threw himself down into a chair.

"Damn nice of you to offer brother!I appreciate it I really do but I don't drink never have don't touch the stuff.It's not that it's bad it's just not my thing not my style not what winds my clock.I'm sure you fine gentlemen understand."

Finding half a second for the first time since he sat down, Captain Estevez said, "Of course Sherman, we understand."

"Hot damn that's great.So how are you brother?How are you doing?How is it going?Is it going well out there brother?Have you been successful lately?"

"Lately it's been interesting."

"Oh man do I ever know that one brother.Life is interesting.Interesting.Absolutely interesting and just when you think you have it figured out BAM!Something comes completely out of the blue and blindsides you!"

Seemingly in one motion, Sherman removed a small tin container from inside his jacket, flipped it open, raised it to his nose, inhaled quickly, opened his eyes wide, snapped shut the container and put it back inside his jacket.

"What was that?" Sausalito asked.

"BROTHER!That was a little fairy dust.Pixie magic.Wake up juice.Oden's nectar.Little burst of stars mixed with rays direct from the sun.It'll make you fly!Live forever!You want a taste?"

Sausalito looked quizzically at Estevez who subtly shook his head. Sausalito thanked Sherman for the offer, but declined.

"Hey I totally understand.You do you brother you do you.I am riding a wave of love to the sandy dunes of paradise."

As quickly as he had arrived, he suddenly stood up, vigorously shook both men's hands and said, "It was great to see you guys again great to see you.Be well my brothers.It's a beautiful night magical.Be well my brothers.Be well.Cats in Hats;stay vigilant."

He was gone before either could say a word in response.

"Captain Estevez! Sausalito! So good to see you my friends!" the proprietor called out as he reached their table.

Rising to their feet, each greeted him warmly. Gesturing for them to follow, he led them out the back door, up a hidden stairwell and onto the roof. There, four tables were arranged facing the water off in the distance. The town glowed in the dark, with the sounds of revelry rising from its streets in all directions.

Opening one of his finest bottles of wine, he filled three glasses. All saluted and drank.

"Thank you Hector. You know, of all the countless establishments on this island, yours is my absolute favorite. There are many I like here, but yours is the best!"

Sausalito echoed the sentiment and Hector profusely thanked them. He reiterated that they were some of his favorite customers and he always looked forward to seeing them.

Pouring fresh glasses, he leaned in and said, "I wish it could all be good times and laughter tonight, but I'm afraid I have some very serious news to share with you. Someone is looking for you."

"We know," Estevez said. "We've already had a run-in with him."

"You have?!"

"He surprised us and killed several of the crew. Managed to fight him off, but I'm sure he will try again. Thank you for letting us know."

"So you already know that he is headed to New Seville to find you?"

"What did you just say?"

"*Si*, he is heading there right now I believe."

"How do you know this!?"

"The individual was in here two days ago asking about you. He was offering gold coins to anyone who knew of your whereabouts, or places you were likely to visit. The idiot was unaware that you and I are friends, and thankfully none of the regulars said anything. However, a drunk at the bar mentioned that he had heard you were spotted on New Seville. After receiving a gold coin, the man insisted the information was accurate. He said you knew the owner of an establishment there called the Crazy Goat, and that's the island you were on."

Estevez and Sausalito shot each other excited looks, then Estevez looked back at Hector and said, "You say this took place two days ago? And the individual is sailing for New Seville as we speak?"

"I'm almost positive. He looked very excited when he heard the man say that he was sure you were there. He yelled at someone with him to prepare the ship for immediate departure. I can't absolutely promise, but it definitely sounded like that's where he was headed."

Estevez thanked Hector for the information, and the three of them drank the last of the fine bottle of wine.

Estevez and Sausalito then apologized for having to depart so suddenly. Hector declared the apology quite unnecessary.

"Find that bastard and send him to Hell! Then come back here and we will celebrate your victory!" he said as they departed.

On the way down to the ship, Estevez declared that he didn't want anything shared with the crew. They had the upper hand now and he didn't want to risk some of them getting cold feet at the prospect of another tangle with the ship that attacked them. He would tell them the real reason that they were headed to New Seville once they were underway. He was convinced they could seize the initiative this time and destroy the man who was relentlessly hunting them. There was an island near New Seville that was similar the one the enemy ship hid behind before attacking them outside of Santa Muerte. Estevez had a hunch that the ship might be found there.

Sharing his hunch with Sausalito, his first mate agreed, although he cautioned him to proceed carefully. They weren't sure where the enemy ship was, and they had to avoid making the mistake of falling into the enemy's trap while trying to spring their own. Estevez nodded, but his eyes shone brightly. Caution was for later; now was the time to go on the offensive!

As the setting sun brought Borracho to life again, Captain Montpellier was finalizing his plans to set off in pursuit of the lost gold of Old Havana. Captain Estevez had just set sail for New Seville to seek out the man who was pursuing him. Two days earlier, Captain Umberland had departed for the Panamanian town of Rojanz with a fresh crew of 50 in his new ship *Vengeance*, pursuing his mutinous former crew.

CHAPTER TWENTY-SEVEN

THE *Royal Victoria* was a passenger vessel that sailed between England and the New World on a regular basis. The ship was commanded by Captain John Dover and had 20 crew and 40 passengers onboard. The ship had been knocked off course by a storm during the voyage to its final destination of Kingston, Jamaica. As the ship sailed back towards it normal route, it passed an uninhabited island.

Two passengers standing by the bow suddenly shouted out that they saw somebody on the island. Grabbing his spyglass, Captain Dover surveyed the island and spotted the figure. The man had a full beard and ragged clothes. His hair was tangled and dirty. He was on his knees, weakly waving at the passing ship.

After surveying the rest of the visible part of the island, the captain determined no one else was in sight and ordered two of the crew to row over and get the stranded figure.

Upon their return, four people helped haul him aboard, as he could barely walk. After giving him some water, they carried him to the one empty room they had onboard and Captain Dover instructed the ship's doctor to do what he could for the man.

The man was delirious and mumbled inaudible words as the doctor made him as comfortable as he could. The man soon fell asleep and the captain ordered a crewmember to watch him and see if he could determine where the man came from when he woke up.

Both the captain and the doctor looked at the unconscious man and noticed the unusual scar on the left side of his face. It was in the shape of a crescent moon that started above his left ear, curved across his cheek and ended near the bottom of his earlobe.

Closing the door, Captain Dover returned to his cabin and made a note in his log about the incident.

As day turned to night, the rescued man drifted in and out of consciousness. Sometimes the crewmember watching him could get a few words out of him. Sometimes it was just gibberish. As the night dragged on, the crewmember became unnerved by the man and left to speak with the captain.

"Enter," Captain Dover said upon hearing the knock on his cabin door.

The crewmember entered and the captain inquired what he wanted.

"I'm here to report on the man we rescued Sir."

"Proceed."

"Well it's difficult to understand him in his condition, but apparently he worked on a merchant ship that sunk in a hurricane. By sheer luck, it seemed to have gone down near the island we rescued him from. I guess the waves threw him onto the island and he's been there ever since. He's near dead Sir."

"Let the doctor determine his condition."

"Aye Sir."

"Anything else."

"Aye Sir," the crewmember said, then fell silent.

After a pause, the captain looked up from the chart he had been reviewing and said, "Well what is it? You look odd; are you alright?"

The crewmember swallowed heavily and with a labored breath said, "Could I trouble you to accompany me Sir? I want to see if he's still saying it. If so, you should hear it."

Casting an uncertain glance at him, Captain Dover finally nodded and instructed him to lead the way.

Opening the door to the cabin, both men looked silently at the man lying unconscious on the bed. Sweat covered his chest and arms.

Captain Dover was about to inquire what it was the man had been saying when suddenly the silence was broken by a deep, hoarse voice. Both men caught their breaths and goosebumps filled their arms as the unconscious figure before them croaked out three words:

"Revenge. Revenge. Revenge."

THE END

Made in the USA
San Bernardino, CA
16 November 2018